THE COURTNEY'S MYSTERIES AND ADVENTURES

TRUTH OR LIES!

Timothy William Lawrence

Copyright © 2024

Tim Lawrence

eBook ISBN: 978-1-963609-24-0
Paperback ISBN: 978-1-963609-25-7
Hardcover ISBN: 978-1-963609-26-4

Dedication

I would like to dedicate this second novel to all those outside of my immediate family who has made such an indelible and profound impact on my life. They have been a huge source of inspiration and strength. Their unwavering support and boundless belief in me have fueled my creative journey. Thank you most of all for keeping me focused on Christ and keeping the main thing, the main thing! I love all of you!

TABLE OF CONTENTS

Acknowledgements

I would like to thank my precious wife of 42 years for her patience, wisdom, and support. She has endured much with this bonehead throughout our years together.

The Bible says in Proverbs 27:17, "As iron sharpens iron, so one person sharpens another."

Thanks to all those who have invested their time, given me constructive comments, driven me to be the best I could be, shared their wisdom, and continued to support me through the years. I'm a rich, rich man because of the relationships God has blessed me with.

Introduction

I began writing this novel in 1994. It was the first one of four to be published. My wife, Vicki, and I had been given the joy of having an amazing daughter. Her name is Courtney. When Courtney was eight years old, her best friend's name was also Courtney, hence the basis of my first four novels.

I'm not sure why I waited so long to pick up my writing again and finish this first novel. The only reason I could give is that the timing was right. I've thoroughly enjoyed putting on paper past events and memories and turning them into novels. It's been quite therapeutic and extremely enjoyable.

I have been in the music ministry and student ministry since 1972. My primary purpose and prayer for publishing my novels are to help pre-teen people to know that they have value and purpose. That God cares about them and everything they are involved in. I want them to know that He is that personal. In fact, so personal that He gave His only Son, Jesus Christ, to die for their sins so that they might experience eternal life and also enjoy a wonderfully rewarding life while on earth.

I hope you and your pre-teen child will enjoy reading about various adventures and mysteries the two Courtney's experienced. May it be an encouragement to you, as a parent, to remember the serious responsibility we have in raising our children to be Godly, respectful, polite, and helpful to others.

Chapter One: Self-Deception 101

"Oh my gosh! I can't stand it when people lie! Why can't they just tell the truth?" Courtney said to Coco over the phone.

"What are you whining about, girl?" Coco asked.

"Billy told me he would give back my *Fortnite: Battle Royale* video game that he borrowed, and he keeps telling me that he just forgets to bring it to me. I found out this morning from his little brother that he stepped on it and broke it. Why didn't he just tell me that in the first place instead of lying?"

"He was probably embarrassed, Court. I'm not defending him because he should have told you, but I can see that might be why he kept making lies about it."

"Still wrong!" Courtney retorted.

"I know. You're right, it is wrong. I get it, Court. I'd be upset, too. What are you going to do now?"

"I'm going to tell him he better buy me another one and soon. I loved that game."

"I think he will do that. Billy has always seemed like a standup guy. I just think he's probably a little nervous to tell you what happened to it."

Calming down a little Courtney responded, "Yeah, maybe you're right. I'd be embarrassed too, I guess."

"Hey, you remember last week when we talked about holding each other accountable to make sure we stayed focused on Christ?" Coco asked.

"Yeah," Courtney answered hesitantly.

"Well, in my quiet time the other day, I read a verse that really threw me for a loop. I actually don't remember reading before. Hang on, let me find it." Coco looked in her cell phone on the You Version Bible App to find the verse. "Here it is. Luke 6:30, *'Give to everyone who asks you, and if anyone takes what belongs to you, do not demand it back.'*"

"Wait a minute, Coco. You really think that verse means I don't have the right to ask Billy to pay me back or get me a new video game that he broke?"

"That's exactly what I asked Steve."

Steve Gibson was the student minister that took Ashton's place, the first student minister that the Courtneys had encountered. Ashton had made a huge impact on their lives and was a real favorite of both girls. They wanted to emulate her in their lives, but she left after getting married to Parker Brantley, a minister in Picayune, Mississippi. They had joined him and his church on a mission project last summer. However, Steve had done an amazing job following her. The Courtneys thought a lot of him as well. He was fresh out of Bible College and had more energy than one person should have. His athletic talents allowed him the opportunity to hang with the students whether they were playing volleyball, basketball, frisbee or any other group activity.

Courtney Lawrence and Courtney Sims had been best friends since they were five years old. To minimize confusion, people called Courtney Lawrence, "Coco" and Courtney Sims just "Courtney." They never were your run-of-the-mill students who stayed inside watching TV shows and playing video games. Instead, they were always outside riding their bikes, rollerblading on sidewalks, or exploring new places. They always seemed to be on an exciting adventure. However, this particular journey would take them down roads they had never experienced before.

"I called him immediately after reading that verse because I was confused about it." Coco continued. "He said that Jesus meant we needed to have a different attitude about the things we own. In other words, if anything of ours gets broken or stolen, we need to think about the person more than the item."

"You're telling me that I shouldn't want my video game back and that Billy doesn't owe me?"

"Again, that's exactly what I asked Steve. He told me that while we have the right to ask back for our item or ask the person to pay us for it, we have to let it go and leave it in the hands of the Lord to speak to that individual. He told me that this particular statement has helped him a lot in life, '*If you own something and can't give it away, then you don't own it, it owns you.*'"

Courtney had her head down and shook it back and forth. "Coco, could you really do that? I mean if someone had broken one of your collectible dolls, could you just say it's no big deal?"

"Probably not, Court, but I'm just saying that we need to try because that's what Jesus said we're supposed to do."

Courtney sighed. "Okay. I'll call Billy and tell him what his little brother told me. I'll ask him to get me another one whenever he can. Sounds like a plan?"

"I think it would be awesome if you can do that. Why don't you call him right now?" Coco suggested.

"Right now?"

"Yeah!"

"Okay. I'll call you right back and let you know what he says."

Still, with some frustration, Courtney asked the Lord to give her the strength to forgive Billy and talk to him politely. She dialed his number and it went to his voicemail when he didn't answer. Courtney went ahead and left her message. "Hi, Billy, it's me, Courtney. I saw your little brother this morning and he told me what happened to my video game. I want you to know that it is okay. Accidents happen. I can always get another one later. See ya." She fell back on her bed, looked at the ceiling, and said, "I couldn't have done that without you, Lord. Thanks." Then she thought to herself, *Bummer! I really loved that game.*

Courtney called Coco back and told her the voice message she left on Billy's cell.

"Amazing, Court. Don't know if I could have done that."

"I couldn't have either except I prayed right before I made the call and asked the Lord to help."

"Really proud of you, girl." Coco remarked.

"Well, thanks for holding me accountable like we said we would do with each other. So, what's on the agenda today?" Courtney asked.

"I dunno. We could get together and play *Fortnite: Battle Royale.*" Coco retorted jokingly.

"Oh, real cute, Coco. You're a real comedian."

"Yeah, that was just wrong on my part," Coco replied.

Courtney could hear her laughing on the phone. "You know I'll get you back for that."

"Oh, I know, I know. You always do."

They both laughed.

"Hey, I know what we could do today," Courtney mentioned. "We haven't been to your uncle's gravel pit lately to ride our bikes."

"Sounds like a plan." Coco responded. "Why don't we pack lunch too?"

"Okay. Meet me here at 10:00?"

"Cya then."

The Courtneys would occasionally ride their bikes to the gravel pit where there were many large and small hills they could ride on. Her uncle didn't mind them being there as long as there were any trucks. There usually weren't any on the weekends. Courtney thought about calling her Dad, but he always said to check with her

Mom, so she went ahead, bypassed her Dad and called her Mom. She said it would be fine. Coco asked her Mom as well. Both their mothers reminded them to watch out for snakes that would sometimes show up there.

Coco arrived at Courtney's house on time. They took off and headed to the gravel pit. They rode through the woods, following a well-traveled path that would take them directly to the pit. Unfortunately, it had rained quite a bit over the last few weeks, keeping them from riding as many hills. They had to be extra careful to not fall or slide into the large pool the rain had made. They rode easily for an hour and a half when Coco yelled, "I'm hungry. Let's eat!"

"Me, too. Race you to the top of the hill with the shed and we'll eat there."

Both the Courtneys got to the top of the hill about the same time. They sat under the shed, pulled out their lunches, and admitted it was a good day of bike riding.

"We've got to come out here more often. I forgot how much fun we have." Coco suggested.

"I know. I love it. Hey, I gotta get back by 2:00 because I've got some yard work Dad told me I had to get done."

"Want some help?" Coco asked.

"Seriously? Heck, yeah! That would be great. But before we leave, let's give Kings Peak a try."

The girls had learned about a real mountain in Utah last year in their geography class that had that name and they started calling the gravel hill that because it was the largest hill in the pit. It was very scary and intimidating.

"I don't know, Court," Coco replied.

"Oh, come on. One time before we leave."

Courtney was always the most daring of the two of them.

"Okay. Let's do it before I chicken out," Coco said.

They both chuckled and rode about three hundred yards up and down smaller slopes and valleys, eventually taking their bikes to the top.

"You ready?" Coco asked.

"As ready as I'll ever be. Sure, looks bigger up here, doesn't it?"

"Sure does. But we can do it."

And with that, Coco was the first to descend. Courtney followed shortly after her.

The ride downhill was refreshing but right before Coco got to the bottom she turned to see where Courtney was. She never should have done that because her front wheel hit a solid rock in the gravel, throwing her off her bike. Courtney saw the whole thing and rode to where she had landed. She stopped near Coco and jokingly said that it was the best spill she'd ever seen. That's when Courtney noticed that Coco wasn't laughing but was crying. She had landed in an awkward position on her left shoulder.

"Court, are you okay? I'm sorry for laughing."

"That's okay, Court. I think I messed up my left shoulder pretty badly. It hurts to move it."

"You mean like you might need to go to the emergency room?"

"I don't know. I'm just gonna to sit here for a moment and see if I can get a little relief."

"Can I do anything?"

"Just stay by my side."

"Always."

They sat together on the moist gravel for a few minutes after which Coco said, "Can you help me get on my bike? We can't be here this late."

Courtney helped Coco up and was able to get her on her bike.

"Do you think you'll be able to ride it?"

"I think so."

The girls were able to maneuver their bikes to the path in the woods and rode to Courtney's house. They went inside and Courtney gave her ibuprofen to help with the pain.

"Do you think you broke something?" Courtney asked.

"Not sure. My left shoulder hurts but I can still lift it, so I don't think I broke anything."

"I think you need to call your Mom to come over and look at it."

"NO!" Coco quickly replied. "If there is really something wrong with it, my parents will probably keep me from going to the church-wide skating party tomorrow night, and I can't miss that."

"Well, you got to tell them, Coco."

"Why? It'll probably be fine by tomorrow."

"Yeah, and the moon might turn into cheese, too."

Coco gave her friend a disgusted look.

"What if it's really injured, Coco? You could make it worse by tomorrow."

Coco knew Courtney was only looking out for her best interest and responded, "Look, I'll tell them tomorrow if it continues to hurt."

"Promise?"

"I promise. I'm gonna head home. Sorry, I can't help you with your yard work."

"Yeah, sure. Anything to get out of helping me. Even hurting your shoulder."

They both chuckled although Coco didn't laugh long. She was more concerned than she was letting on.

"See ya in the morning at the church." Coco passed a weak smile.

"Okay, Crip. See ya in the morning. And really, I'll be praying it gets better."

"Thanks, Court."

Coco couldn't sleep at all because her pain hadn't subsided much, if any. She thought about telling her parents but didn't want to miss the skating party. She took another ibuprofen and got dressed for church.

"You're running a little slow this morning, Coco. Hurry and eat your breakfast so we won't be late for church."

"Yes ma'am."

When Coco picked up a gallon-sized milk carton to pour milk into her cereal bowl, she flinched from the soreness.

Her Mom caught her wincing and asked. "Are you okay?"

"Yes ma'am."

"Well, it looked funny when you picked up the milk."

"I just grabbed it wrong and twisted my fingers."

"Oh, okay." Her Mom wasn't buying it, but she let it go. "I guess you're going to the big skating party tonight?"

"Yes ma'am. Wouldn't miss it for anything."

Coco hated the thought that she wasn't being completely truthful with her mom. Vicki was always her biggest cheerleader and encouraged her to always be the best at whatever she was doing. Coco knew she should tell her what had happened but then she remembered the skating party and that thought won.

"Good morning, all!" Coco's Dad hollered louder than normal trying to scare both her and her Mom. Coco's dad was a constant jokester and she loved it. One time she and her dad pranked her mom one April Fool's day. They put a bucket of fake spiders above a door which had a string tied to the door handle on the other side. When Vicki opened it up, the bucket spilled all over her and the neighbors three doors down probably heard her. Coco and her dad were watching the whole time and couldn't stop laughing. Vicki smiled, acting as if it was no big deal and went about her business. She got them back, however, the next week. After supper she asked them if they would like some Oreos for dessert. Tim and Coco loved Oreos and told her absolutely. They both chomped down and swallowed the first cookie before they noticed something very strange in their taste buds. They looked at Vicki and she cracked up. She had replaced the white cream between the cookies with toothpaste. Coco and her dad had been snookered for sure.

Coco chuckled and would have laughed more but the pain was just not subsiding and that was all that was on her mind. Vicki gave Tim a look that could melt butter. She wasn't particularly fond of being scared, but Tim would do it from time to time anyway. He was always joking around, and Coco loved it. One time they were all eating spaghetti, which was his favorite and she looked over at her Dad. He had one strand of a spaghetti noodle hanging out of his mouth. He looked at Vicki and said, "I love eating worms. They are my favorite food."

Vicki quipped back with a grin, "You better straighten up or next time I really will serve you worms. You're such a goober."

"A toys-r-us kid, but you still love me!" he replied back with a huge grin.

Coco hurried with her cereal and wanted to get away from any further interrogation about how she was feeling.

"Well, I'm going to finish getting ready."

"Okay. We'll leave in about fifteen minutes." Her Dad responded.

They got to church on time. Tim and Vicki went to their couple's class and Coco went to the girls' Bible study class. Anna Applin taught the class, and the girls loved it and her. Anna was not only a wonderful teacher but she also tried her best to be as involved as she could in the girl's various activities, like recitals, sports and plays. Courtney was already seated, and Coco sat beside her.

"How's the shoulder?" Courtney whispered.

"Okay."

"I think you might be telling a little white lie. I saw you grimace when you sat down," Courtney admitted.

"Okay, it hurts, but I'll be fine."

"Coco, you really need to tell your parents."

Ms. Applin asked the girls to settle down for Bible study. Good timing for Coco. She didn't want any more questions about the shoulder.

"This morning we're going to read a passage from 1 Corinthians 3:18. Let's turn to it and see what it says. *Do not deceive yourselves. If any of you think you are wise by the standards of this age, you should become "fools" so that you may become wise."* This phrase, 'deceiving yourself' is interesting. I think what Paul was telling the Corinthian Christians was that it's easy to talk ourselves into believing something that isn't particularly true. For instance, you tell your parents you are going to the mall to hang out with some friends. You do go to the mall, but after you've been there for a few minutes, you and your friends go joyriding around. It's what I call a half-truth or deceiving yourself into believing what you told your parents was completely true. Another example would be that your parents want you to join them to go out to eat but you say that you really need to get your homework done for the next day. You stay and actually study for about ten minutes and then you get on your cell phone. Again, a half-truth. You made yourself believe that what you told your parents was totally true." Coco was not only squirming in her seat because of her shoulder pain but also because the Holy Spirit was dealing with her about her not telling her parents about her injury. Every now and then Courtney eyed Coco wondering if she was getting this. Coco raised her hand. Ms. Applin nodded at her.

"So, are you saying that we need to tell every little detail of our lives to the person or people involved in a given situation?"

Anna grinned and said, "Boy, Coco, you must have thought long and hard on that one. That's a really good question and one I hope I can give an answer to that will help you all understand. Let's say something has happened to you. Something you did. Or perhaps, someone else did it to you. It's hurting you emotionally, mentally, physically, or spiritually, and most likely, you know deep down that you should tell someone about it. Every child of God who has the Holy Spirit in them will receive a nudge from Him letting them know what they should do. That's a short answer for a deep question, but does it make sense to everyone?"

Everyone shook their heads, except Coco. She just put her head down and looked at the floor. Anna noticed it, too.

"Well, that was the bell. What a good discussion today. I pray that we'll take what we learned this morning and use it outside these church walls and not live in that big town of 'self-denial'. Let's pray."

After prayer, Anna dismissed the girls and asked Coco for a moment.

"Yes ma'am," Coco answered.

"Are you okay? You seem to have something on your mind this morning."

"Oh, no ma'am. I'm fine."

"Okay. You know you can always talk to me if you're struggling with anything."

"Yes ma'am. Thank you."

All the girls had left the room and went to get a drink of water or use the restroom before going into the sanctuary for the worship service. Courtney grabbed Coco by her arm and asked if she was okay. She looked at Courtney and told her she was fine. Courtney knew better but didn't push it for now.

The service was awesome! It usually was at Christ Community Church which both Lawrence and Sims attended. The praise team led the congregation in three inspiring songs. Melissa Worthy sang 'Fearless' by Jasmine Murray. Whenever she sang, you could feel the presence of the Lord. Then their pastor Kenny Parker, aka KP as their church called him gave a challenging message on the same song, 'Fearless'. Coco was visibly miserable the whole time. Her shoulder was aching and so was her heart. She thought again about telling her parents but knew it would most likely mean her not going to the skating party. The service ended and Courtney slid over to Coco.

"I can tell you're hurting really bad."

"I'm fine," Coco snapped back uncharacteristically. "Quit bothering me about it."

"Okay, okay. Sorry!"

Coco looked at Courtney and said, "Sorry. I'll see you at the skating rink tonight." She then turned away, got into her parent's car, and waited for them. They always talked to many of the folks at church after the service. Normally, it never bothered Coco, but she was ready to get home, get a couple of Tylenols in her system, and lay down for a while. They finally came out and discussed the service on the way home. Coco's parents sensed something different about their daughter because usually, she would give her two cents about the wonderful service.

"You okay, sweet?" her Dad asked.

"Yessir."

"Okay. You just seem a little down."

"No. I'm good."

All that was going on in Coco's head was the Sunday Bible class. In her head, she was saying over and over, "Self-deceiver. Half-truths. Loser." The devil was doing a number on her. That was for sure.

Coco's Mom thought it was odd that her daughter stayed in her room all Sunday afternoon. It was rare that she did that but again, she thought she'd give her some space. She thought she'd eventually tell her or Tim if there was a problem. She always did. Coco got some rest because the Tylenol kicked in a little relief. She got up from her bed and got dressed to go to the party. She found her Dad in his favorite recliner watching the news. He always watched the news.

"Dad, could you run me to the skating rink?"

"No, but I can take you in the car." He stared at her with that look like, "I just made a clever joke."

She just looked at him like he just made a bad 'Dad' joke.

"Sure, sweet. Let me get my shoes on."

She was about to walk out the door when her Mom touched her left shoulder to kiss her bye. Coco winced and her Mom noticed.

"Coco, I didn't mean to grab you so hard. I was trying to give you a kiss before you left."

"No, Mom. You didn't hurt me. You just caught me off guard because I didn't see you coming around the door."

"Well, I thought it was weird how you jumped when I touched you."

Coco gave a quick response to keep from any more conversing. "Love you, Mom. Dad is outside waiting for me."

"Love you, too, honey. Have a great time. Break a leg…wait. Don't do that."

They both chuckled a little. Still, the voices inside her head were rattling Coco's brain. Her Dad dropped her off at the rink.

"Have a rock and roll time, sweet."

"I will, Dad. Love you."

"Love you, too."

She was sick to her stomach. She was not only continuing to deceive herself, but she'd basically been deceiving her parents since the accident happened. Courtney saw her and ran over to her.

"Can you believe how many are here tonight? There's got to be at least five hundred people."

"Yeah, at least. Let's get our skates," Coco responded unenergetically.

They walked to the counter and picked up their skates. Once they had them on, they immediately hit the floor and started skating. It was clearly a madhouse. There had to be two or three hundred on the skating rink. Others were playing video games, eating, or just hanging out. Coco's shoulder was still giving her fits, but the skating seemed to help keep her mind off it. That's until a kid named Bobby from their church, who was a couple of years older and always a pest, rolled right in between the Courtneys. He was just going to nudge them as a joke. He didn't mean to hit them as hard as he did.

All three of them fell to the floor. Unfortunately, Coco fell directly on her left shoulder. The pain was immense, to say the least. She did all she could to not scream out. Their student minister happened to see the fall and ran onto the floor to check on them. Bobby apologized and said he didn't mean to hit them and that he was just playing around. Courtney said she was fine, but then pointed to Coco, who was still sitting on the floor holding her left shoulder. Steve knelt down in front of her and asked, "Coco, are you okay?"

"I'm not sure. I might have injured my shoulder," She replied quietly.

"You probably messed it up more from the…"

"I'll be fine. I just need to find a place to chill for a minute or so." Coco interrupted before Courtney could finish.

Steve said, "You're sure?"

"Yeah. I'll be fine. Thanks."

Courtney glared hard and long at her. When Steve walked away Courtney bashed, "You can get mad all you want at me, but I believe it's time you quit playing this little charade and do something about your shoulder."

Coco didn't make eye contact with Courtney but knew she was correct. She pulled out her cell phone and called her parents and asked them to pick her up. She told them what happened, and her Dad immediately drove there to get her.

Steve met Coco's Dad at the door of the rink and told him he was sorry for what had happened to Coco.

"Thanks, Steve, but it wasn't anyone's fault, really. Things like this happen and I'm sure her shoulder will be okay."

"Let me know later, Coco, how you're feeling."

"Okay. Thanks again."

As she and her Dad were walking to their car, he told her he thought it would be best to go to the doc-in-the-box and get her shoulder checked out.

"I'm fine, Dad, really."

"Well, let's just be sure."

He called Vicki and told her what they were going to do, and she agreed that it was the wisest thing. He drove to the nearest medical facility and checked her in. They sat in the waiting area for about an hour then a nurse told her that she could come back with her. After a few minutes, the doctor walked into the room where Coco was and introduced himself, asking her what happened. She told him and he began examining her left shoulder, trying to assess the severity of her injury.

"It appears that you have severely strained your shoulder, maybe even separated it. Let's do a couple of X-rays and that will give us more precise information." The doctor left the room and went into the waiting area.

"Are you the father of the young girl with the injured shoulder?"

"Yessir," Tim answered.

"We're going to take a couple of X-rays to get a more detailed look at her shoulder. Was she already having complications with it?"

"No, I don't think so. If she was, she didn't tell me or my wife. Why do you ask?"

"I have difficulty understanding how the injury that happened would have caused such damage. I believe it has a considerable separation. Had she recently injured her left shoulder prior to the skating incident?"

Coco's Dad answered, "No, not that I'm aware of, Doctor."

"The X-rays will, of course, tell us more. You're welcome to join her in the room."

"Thanks, doc." The doctor took him to her room and told her a nurse would be with her shortly to take her to the X-ray room. "

"Sweet, you, okay?" Tim asked.

"Yeah, Dad. Just hurting really bad."

"Sorry. Hey, umm, just wondering…The doctor told me just now that he was surprised that your shoulder got injured that badly with just the fall from skating. Did you happen to have hurt it earlier?"

Coco had had enough. She looked at the floor and started crying.

"Sweet, what's wrong?"

Tim brought her close to him and gently hugged her, making sure he wasn't touching her left shoulder. She got some control of her emotions and through some more crying and sniffling she began, "Dad, I'm so sorry. I've been hiding something from you and Mom since Saturday afternoon." Her Dad didn't interrupt and waited for her to tell everything to him. She told him the whole story and how she fell off her bike going down King's Peak.

"Sweet, why didn't you tell us?"

"I knew that you probably wouldn't let me go to the skating party."

"Baby, they'll be many, many more skating parties but there's only one of you and you're way too special to not let us know when you are having any issues, whether they're physical, emotional, or spiritual. We want to always be there for you and, yes, sometimes parents have to make tough decisions that aren't very popular with their children, but they're for their best."

"Yeah, I know, Dad. I'm a bonehead."

"Well, sure you are, but you've always been that." He gave her a gentle hug and a huge smile.

The nurse walked in and took her to get her X-rays. Sure enough, the shoulder had a severe separation and it most likely wouldn't have been near as severe if Coco had done something about it earlier. A lesson learned, for sure. There wasn't much that could be done for the injury except put her arm in a sling to reduce the pain and take stronger medicine to reduce the inflammation. Hopefully, the seriousness won't mean surgery. Coco kept thinking to herself, "Self-deceiving yourself and everyone else didn't do you any good, did it? You're such a goober." They arrived home and the whole story was retold by Coco with many apologies to boot. Tim and Vicki didn't think she needed any punishment for her lying and misleading them. They believed that she learned a tremendous lesson and thanked the Lord for how He moved in her life with this episode. They knew there would be other lessons to discover in her life and hoped this one she would learn from and not repeat.

Coco realized she needed to call her best friend and apologize to her as well. She dialed Courtney's number.

"Hey, Court."

"Hey, you. Glad you called. How are you feeling?"

"I'm okay but I needed to talk to you and let you know that I'm so sorry about how I've been acting toward you lately. I let this shoulder thing get me way out of joint. I still can't believe I was basically lying to you, my parents, and everyone else about it. I'm such a jerk!"

"Coco, look, we all have those times where we let situations take control of us. No biggie! You know, I Love ya, but if you ever lie to me again, I'll have to take you out. That's just what I do."

They both chuckled.

"Seriously, though, Court," Coco continued soberly, "I really am sorry. I hope I never do anything like that again. I really can't understand it. I think Ms. Applin really hit on it. I was living in the big town of 'self-denial'. After my Dad and I got home I went to my room and did some digging for more info on that subject. Check this verse out. 1 Peter 3:10 *'For, whoever would love life and see good days must keep their tongue from evil and their lips from deceitful speech.'* I put it up on my mirror in my bedroom. Don't want no lips from deceitful speech."

"Me neither! I'm highlighting that one in my Bible right now, too. 1 Peter 3:10?" Courtney asked.

"Yep!"

"Got it. Thanks."

"Why don't you come over to my house tomorrow? We'll figure out some kind of trouble to get into." Courtney laughed.

"Sounds good. I'll see ya at about 10:00 am, but no gravel pits." They both snickered. After their conversation, Coco walked into the kitchen. Her Mom was sitting on the couch in the den, reading a novel by Joel C. Rosenberg called 'The Last Jihad.' Tim was watching the news as usual. She asked them if it was okay to go to Courtney's home tomorrow and hang out. They said that would be fine but to check in every now and then.

"How's the shoulder this morning?" Vicki asked.

"It's pretty sore, still. The doctor said it will be like that for a few days."

"Did you take any pain medicine?"

"Yes, ma'am. Twelve Advils."

Vicki looked at Coco with total disbelief. Coco snickered. Coco walked up to her Mom, gave her a big hug, and then gave her Dad one as well.

"I really do love you two. Again, I'm so sorry for not being honest with you and Dad."

"Sweetheart, we all mess up every now and then. That's understandable and as long as we learn from the ordeal, we make a positive resolve from it, and then ask the Lord to keep us from that in the future, we're good."

Coco smiled and told them she was going to bed.

Chapter Two: Courtney's Relatives

Coco didn't sleep very well because of her shoulder. Every time she would turn to her left side, the pain would wake her up. She laid there for a little longer and decided to get up. She went into the kitchen to eat some cereal where she saw her Mom having her quiet time at the dinner table, which was always an encouragement to Coco.

"Hey, Mom."

"Hey, honey. Can I fix you something?"

"No ma'am. I'm just going to have some Cinnamon Toast cereal."

"How's the arm this morning?"

"The same."

"Sorry."

"Thanks, Mom."

After Coco finished her second bowl of cereal she went to her bedroom and got dressed to hang out with Courtney. She kissed her Mom goodbye and jumped on her bike. She saw Courtney in their backyard sitting on their patio furniture, so she rode through the ditch and pulled onto their patio.

"Whatcha' doing?" Coco asked.

"My Mom just told me that her sister Candi called and asked if she and her daughter could stay next week with us. Their house burned down in a fire, and they need a place to stay until they can land somewhere else. They lived in a mobile home, and they think the wiring caught on fire or something like that. Their insurance couldn't place them anywhere until next week after they've done a full investigation."

Coco stared at her best friend and said, "That is so sad! Their house burned down! Wow! Did they lose everything?"

"I think Mom said they were able to get some of their clothes and other useful items out before it totally burned."

"That has to be a serious bummer when your home burns down," Coco said.

"For real," Courtney countered. Your clothes, games, jewelry, TV, furniture, appliances, and keepsakes. Everything gone up in flames!"

"Have I ever met your Aunt's family?" Coco asked.

"I don't think so. They live in Tupelo. We hardly ever see them. Mom's sister got a divorce about a year ago and according to Mom, her ex-husband never comes to see them or helps with any money issues. My Aunt works part-time at Walmart and cleans houses on the side to make ends meet. I think Mom said her business was called 'Clean Up with Candi.'"

Coco asked how many children they had.

"She has a daughter named Lexi. I think she's about 16 years old. I've only seen her a couple of times in three or four years. When we would go on vacation to Tennessee we would always drop by and say hi. We never stayed overnight so I really don't know her that well."

"When are they coming?" Coco inquired.

"I think Mom said they'd be here tomorrow," Courtney paused. "Hey, to change the subject, you're never going to believe this, but Billy said he needed to come by the house today and see me."

"What? Billy?"

"Yeah, I know. I'm glad you're going to be here because I don't want to get into an argument or anything with him. You know, I haven't heard from him since I left him that voicemail on his phone."

Right at that moment the doorbell rang. Both girls looked at each other with curiosity. Courtney walked to the door as Coco walked into the other room. She opened the door and, in the doorway, stood Billy with his hands behind his back.

"Hi, Billy. You want to come in?"

"Nah. Thanks. I just needed to see you for a minute."

"What about?"

Billy held out his hand holding a brand new *Fortnite: Battle Royale* video game to replace the one he broke a couple of weeks ago. "I'm really sorry I wasn't straight with you about your game. I was an idiot."

"No, you weren't an idiot. It just surprised me that you wouldn't tell me the real reason why you hadn't given it back. I would have understood. But I understand how you could be embarrassed too. We've all been there before."

"Well, I wanted to give you this and say I'm sorry again."

"Billy, this wasn't necessary. I really wish you hadn't bought me another one," Courtney said, looking at the game.

"That was the least I could do. After you left the voice message telling me that you knew what happened and for me not to worry about the game, it really got to me. Well, I should say, the Lord really got to me. I felt horrible for lying to you and continuing to give you the run-around. Well, I've got to get to work, so I'll talk to you later."

"Okay. Maybe we can get some friends together and have a Fortnite challenge," Courtney suggested, taking the game.

"That would be great!" Billy retorted.

"See ya and thanks again, Billy." He waved back as he rode away on his bike.

Coco came back into the living room and Courtney looked at her. "Can you believe this? Billy bought me the video game that he broke. How cool is that?"

"Pretty cool," Coco replied.

"I know," Courtney said with excitement. "He said the Lord convicted him and he had to make it right."

"I can relate to that for sure," Coco answered.

Both girls giggled knowing that Coco was referring to her most recent spiritual struggle.

The next morning Courtney's parents, Ralph and Melinda, were sitting at the breakfast table discussing how they would manage the next week with her sister's family being there. "Thanks, Honey, for being so willing to have Candi and Lexi stay with us this week," Melinda said.

"Well, it's the least we could do. I'd sure appreciate someone helping us out if our house burned down," Ralph responded.

"Oh, I hope we never have to go through anything like that. It would be horrible," she paused. "They should be here within an hour. She texted a few minutes ago and said they had stopped in the city of Winona for a restroom break."

As they were talking, Candi and Lexi pulled into their driveway. Courtney and her parents met them at the door and invited them in. They hugged each other awkwardly since they had never been around each other for more than a couple of hours every time they visited. Candi was a couple of years younger than Melinda, had the same bright red colored hair that her mom had and slightly shorter in height. She looked exhausted and distraught and rightfully so with what they had recently experienced. Lexi was tall with beautiful long auburn colored hair and looked very athletic. She never made any eye contact with Courtney's family.

They gathered in the family room and conversed about the extent of the fire, what they lost, and the details about their insurance. It truly was a sad situation. They lost most of everything they owned. Thank goodness they had insurance, or it really would have been a total disaster.

"I'll whip up some sandwiches for lunch. Ralph, would you mind showing them the guest room?" Melinda said.

"Be glad to. Follow me." Ralph grabbed a couple of their suitcases to the guest bedroom.

Courtney went to help her Mom with lunch. As she was getting the mayonnaise and mustard out of the refrigerator, she quietly whispered to her Mom, "This is going to be a little weird, Mom."

Melinda looked to make sure they weren't being overheard and said, "Yeah, it will be a little strange. It always is when you have relatives or friends around who are not routinely with you, but we need to be there for them right now."

"I know you're right, Mom. I'm just hoping me and Lexi will get along."

"Oh, I'm sure you two will be thick as thieves before this week is over."

Courtney wasn't so sure about that.

In the room, Ralph turned to Candi and said, "Candi, I'm sorry we only have one bed. I guess you two could sleep in it together, but we do have the couch in the family room and it's pretty comfy."

"Thanks, Ralph. We'll figure out what we're going to do later." Candi answered.

"Okie dokie!"

Melinda called for everyone to come into the kitchen and grab a ham or turkey sandwich, chips, and a drink. Everyone got some food off of the bar and pulled a chair up to the table. Lexi had already started eating when Ralph spoke up, "Hold on, y'all. Let's thank the Lord for this stuff. Father, thank You for who You are and what You do for us every day. Thank you, especially for keeping Candi and Lexi safe during the fire. And thank You for the food we're about to eat. In Jesus' name, amen." Courtney took a peek and noticed Lexi didn't close her eyes and continued chomping down on her sandwich.

After everyone ate their sandwiches, they enjoyed some leftover coconut pie that Melinda had made earlier in the week but there wasn't much conversation. Seemed like Candi and Lexi were all talked out. Ralph was the first to excuse himself from the table saying he needed to get some yard work done. Candi told Melinda that she would help clean up, which left Courtney and Lexi to themselves. Awkward! Courtney looked at Lexi and asked if she wanted to go to her room. Lexi gave her a nonchalant nod. They walked in and Courtney flopped down on her large bean bag. Lexi just walked around the room looking at all of the pictures on the wall, the different video games on her shelf and the other paraphernalia in Courtney's room.

"So, what do you all do around here for fun?" Lexi asked.

"Mostly ride bikes, explore the woods, play video games a little, and other junk like that."

"Hmm." Lexi showed little interest. "So, you got any friends?"

"Oh, sure. My best friend is Courtney Lawrence and I have a bunch of other friends at the church we attend."

"Courtney, huh? Isn't that sweet? The same name as yours. And you said you had friends from your church?"

"Yeah."

"Church! Now that's one place you won't find me. The way I see it, the church is basically for people who can't handle life. They have to have some sort of crutch and, well, the church is their crutch."

"I could see that, but the church is much more than that to me. It's a place where I go to learn more about Jesus and how I can live like Him."

"Uh oh! You're one of those holy rollers, I guess," Lexi responded with a twisted facial expression.

"Yeah. Guilty as charged, that is if you mean I'm a Christian." Courtney retorted.

"How old are you, Courtney?"

"Just about to turn thirteen."

"Yeah, that makes sense. I give you another couple of years and you'll see that church, Jesus, and all that stuff is bogus. You'll realize it soon enough."

"Lexi, I asked Christ to come into my life when I was ten. Needless to say, I didn't have any horrible issues or gross sinful habits in my life but knew when I gave Him my life, He saved me for eternity and took all my sins away…past, present, and future. Got to tell ya, He's made all the difference in my life. Just don't see me changing that belief in a couple of years or ever."

"You will. Trust me. When life begins to hit you, all that stuff will begin to just crumble right out from under your feet," Lexi replied with a sly grin.

Lexi quickly switched gears and said, "I saw a basketball goal on your driveway. You shoot hoops?"

"Yeah, not very good but I like to every now and then."

"Let's go." They went directly to the garage and Lexi grabbed the basketball. She took a couple of shots and made both of them.

"Wow! You're pretty good, Lexi."

"Yeah. I play guard on the varsity team back home. I scored fifteen points in one of our games last year."

"Nice! I just don't have the skill but still like to play the game," Courtney confessed.

Lexi chunked the ball at Courtney and almost knocked her down.

"Shoot, Courtney. Let's see what you got."

Courtney took a shot and missed. Lexi bent over and laughed really hard. Courtney was embarrassed, and chased down the ball, taking another shot. This time it hits the rim.

"Well, you hit the rim, at least. Throw it here."

Courtney did and Lexi dribbled the ball in between her legs and up to the goal and put in the nicest layup you'd ever seen.

"Now, that's how you do it, Cuz."

Courtney wasn't looking when Lexi threw the ball at her again. And it came flying right to her head. It hit her so hard that it slammed her to the ground. With no apology, Lexi looked down at her.

"You gotta always be looking, Courtney. You never know when the ball is gonna be coming to you."

Courtney's Dad came around the corner at that same time and saw Courtney on the ground. "You okay, sweet?"

Courtney wanted to tell her Dad that Lexi was basically a pompous, snobby jerk and she just knocked me down to the ground with a hard-thrown basketball, but she held off and just said, "I'm good. Lexi and I are just playing a little basketball."

"Throw me the ball, Lexi," Ralph said.

Lexi tossed him the ball and Ralph took a three-point shot that went right through the hoop. "Now that's what I'm talking about Courtney. That's the way to shoot," Lexi admired.

"Thanks, Lexi. Appreciate it," Tim responded and thought to himself, "I still got it" and then laughed within himself.

Still on the ground and her head ringing from the ball hitting her, Courtney's cell rang. She answered it. It was Coco. She walked a couple of yards from the game as Lexi continued shooting the basketball.

"Hey!"

"Hey yourself. What are you doing?" Coco asked.

"Shooting hoops with Lexi."

"Sounds like it's going well with them there."

"Well, I guess you could say that," Courtney replied.

"You don't sound convincing."

"I'll talk to you later about it. Maybe at church."

"Okay. Hang in there."

"Who was that?" Lexi asked.

"My best friend."

"She plays ball?"

"About like I do."

"Sad. You two need to get a life."

Courtney wanted to respond but chose not to. She was getting a little frustrated and didn't want to get upset. "I think I'm gonna go inside and get cleaned up," Courtney told Lexi.

"Whatever," Lexi responded.

Courtney went inside, took a shower, and got ready for bed. It was only 9:30 pm but she was ready to get away from Lexi and any further drama. She was sitting on her bed when her Mom came in.

"You're going to bed this early?"

"Yes ma'am. Is that okay?"

"Do you feel okay? You're not sick, are you?"

"No ma'am. Just a little tired, I guess."

She kissed Courtney's forehead and told her to sleep well. Courtney lay there for a while, thinking about how long the week was going to be. She started praying and asking the Lord to give her the wisdom and endurance to handle whatever happened. She asked Him to help her be the best witness that she could be so Lexi would see Jesus in her life. She was reminded of an alliteration that Steve told them to pursue. It was on a wall hanging at the front of the room. It read, the 'A.A.R.T.T.' of Christianity. The alliteration was: Attitude of Christ, Actions of Christ, the Reactions of Christ, the Thoughts of Christ, and the Talk of Christ. He told the students to live out the A.A.R.T.T. of Christianity, which could only be done with the power of the Holy Spirit.

Courtney continued praying, "Father, help me to do just that every day but especially this week while Lexi is here. It's gonna be difficult but I know through your strength, I can do it. I pray that Lexi would see you reflected in my life and even come to know you."

"Good morning, Candi," said Melinda. "I made some breakfast for everyone this morning. I didn't know if you two were morning people or not."

"Wow! Eggs, bacon, toast, and cinnamon rolls too. You went all out, sis."

"Thanks. I try to do it on Sunday before we head to church to start the morning out right."

"Sure, looks and smells great. I'll go see if Lexi wants some. She normally doesn't eat anything in the morning."

Candi went back to the guest room and attempted to wake Lexi up, but she wanted to stay in bed.

"You're gonna miss out, girl. Your Aunt fixed eggs, bacon, toast, and even homemade cinnamon rolls."

"Go away. I wanna sleep."

"Okay, okay," Candi responded letting her daughter remain dead to the world.

"Ooh, Mom. It smells so good. Thanks for cooking," Courtney told her Mom.

"You're welcome, honey. Will you get the milk out of the fridge?"

"Sure," Ralph snuck up behind Melinda, grabbing her around her waist and kissing her cheek. That was his way of saying thanks for breakfast. Ralph got everyone's attention and asked them to join him in thanks for the grub. After the prayer, Melinda told everyone to grab a plate and dig in. Then she said to Candi, "Y'all are more than welcome to go to church with us this morning if you want to."

"Thanks, sis, but we'll pass. We don't really do the church thing anymore. Just ain't for us."

Ralph jumped into the conversation. "No problem, Candi. We just wanted y'all to know you were welcome."

"Okie dokie," Candi coolly replied.

Ralph and Melinda thought it best to leave that conversation where it was, at least for the time being. They both would continue praying that they would be a Godly influence on her and Lexi while they were at their house.

Ralph yelled, "Let's go, Court. We're gonna be late as it is."

"Yessir. I'm coming." Courtney and her parents left Candi and Lexi at their home while they went to church. They chatted on the way there that the week was going to be somewhat of a struggle, but the Lord must have a purpose in it. Once they arrived at church, they went to their Bible study classes. Coco saw Courtney in the parking lot and hollered at her.

"Well, Coco asked, how was it yesterday with your Aunt and Lexi?"

"Little weird," Courtney answered with a scrunched-up expression.

"Whatcha mean?"

"I dunno. Lexi is just different. She seems to think a lot about herself. Kind of brags a little. Also, she puts down Christians."

"Really? What did she say?"

"She said Jesus and all that stuff was for people who couldn't stand up for themselves. I just told her church was much more than that to me. That it was a place where I go to learn more about Jesus and how I can live like Him. I told her about me getting saved when I was ten."

"Really, cool, Court. How did she respond to that?"

"She changed the subject. We then went outside and started shooting the basketball. She's good and made sure I knew it. She threw the ball at me when I wasn't looking, so hard that it knocked me down. I'm pretty sure it was intentional."

"Gosh, I am so sorry, Court."

"Ahh, it's only for a week. It'll be okay. Let's get to class."

They got to their Bible class on time. They couldn't wait to hear what Ms. Anna Applin was going to teach. Coco even found a moment to apologize to Ms. Applin for the dishonest response she gave her last Sunday. Anna told her she understood and that she didn't need to worry about it. Ralph and Melinda were in their class and during the prayer request time, they asked the class to remember them this week and the situation with Melinda's family.

Bible classes were great as usual, and the church service was very uplifting. The Courtneys said goodbye to each other and promised to call. Courtney's family's attitude was better going home than coming to church. They were sure that the Lord had brought Candi and Lexi to their home for a purpose, and they were going to trust Him to use them in whatever way He wanted.

Chapter Three: Cousin Lexi

When they reached home, they walked in with their newly found purpose but what they saw took a lot of the wind out of their sails. They found one empty beer can on the table and Candi downing another one. Apparently, she had gone out and purchased a six-pack. The sight took all three of them by surprise, but they were able not to show it.

"Well, how was church?" Candi asked as she continued watching an HGTV rerun where Chip and Joanna Gaines had just finished beautifully refurbishing another house in Waco.

"It was wonderful. Wish you and Lexi had come. I think you would have really enjoyed it," Melinda answered her sister. "This morning's service centered around how Christians need to be more real. How often times they can put on a show and be hypocritical. The drama team did a skit that was hilarious and did a great job getting the point across."

Candi, still looking at the TV, replied uninterestingly, "Well, good for y'all."

"Well, I'm gonna whip up some lunch for us. Chili sound good?" Melinda asked, changing the topic.

"Sure. Whatever," Candi responded indifferently.

When Courtney got to her bedroom, she found Lexi laying on her bed, rummaging through her most recent school annual.

"Dude! Who is this guy? He is super fine."

Courtney took a look and told her she didn't know him. They didn't really associate with students who were much older than them.

"Well, I'd sure like to meet him. I'd make sure he would remember me if you know what I mean."

Courtney ignored the remark as she was putting up her clothes. While replacing her necklace, she noticed one of her favorite rings was missing from her jewelry tree. She looked at the floor but didn't see it anywhere. She asked Lexi if she'd seen it.

"What ring? Why would I have seen it? Is it one you got out of a Cracker Jack's box?" Lexi laughed like that was the greatest joke she'd ever heard.

Courtney didn't find the humor in her snide remark and replied, "No, actually it was one of my favorite rings. My grandmother Mimi gave it to me when I was eight."

"It'll show up somewhere. No biggie."

Courtney couldn't hold it in. Her annoyance with Lexi got the best of her.

"Well, it's a biggie to me, Lexi. The ring has a lot of sentimental value to me. So, yeah, it's a big deal to me. Thanks for caring!"

"Whoa, cowboy! Don't be coming to me with an attitude. I didn't lose the ring. You need to back down."

"Shut up, Lexi. In fact, get out of my room, and don't ever come in here unless I'm in here."

Lexi stood for a moment looking at Courtney, took a step toward her as if she were going to hit her but then turned and walked out the door. Courtney shut the door harder than she meant to. She got on her hands and knees and looked everywhere in her room for her grandmother's ring but to no avail. She started crying over the loss of the ring, but more significantly because of her reaction and anger towards Lexi. At that same moment, her cell rang. It was Coco.

"Hello."

"Hey, girl. What are you doing?"

"I just blew it with Lexi."

"Tell me what happened?"

"We came home from church, and she was in my room looking at one of the school annuals. I noticed that one of my favorite rings was missing from my jewelry tree. I looked everywhere for it, and she made some smart-mouth remarks that just ticked me off really badly."

"What happened then?"

"I smarted off back to her and told her to get out and not come into my room again unless I'm there."

"Do you think she took the ring?"

"I didn't even think about that, Coco. Gosh, I hope not."

Now Courtney was concerned about the possibility of Lexi stealing the ring instead of it being lost.

"It's probably in your room somewhere. You want me to come over and help you look for it?" Coco suggested, trying to calm her.

"I'd love for you to, but I guess I better go make amends with Lexi."

"Okie dokie. I'll see you tomorrow."

"Okay, bye."

Courtney slowly walked out of her room looking for Lexi to apologize to her. She saw her outside shooting some hoops, so she went outside to talk to her.

"Hey, Lexi."

"What do you want? You gonna tell me to not shoot basketball unless you are here?" Lexi answered while continuing to shoot the basketball.

"I'm sorry I snapped at you like I did. I was just upset about not finding my ring."

Lexi didn't stop nor make any eye contact. "Yeah, whatever."

Courtney didn't know what to do next.

"Can I take a couple of shots with you?"

She threw the ball at Courtney. "I'm through. You can play all you want."

Thank goodness her Mom called everyone and told them that lunch was ready, although she wasn't in any mood to eat. Courtney prayed that the Lord would give her wisdom and compassion. It's only been one day and it's already a mess, Courtney thought to herself.

They all sat down and started eating after the blessing. Lexi was not there.

Ralph asked, "Where's Lexi, Candi?"

"She said she wasn't hungry. She had some of the leftovers from breakfast when she finally got up."

"Court, What grade are you in now?" Candi asked.

"I'll be in the seventh this year."

"I didn't realize Lexi was that much older than you. She's fifteen but she flunked last year so she'll be in the ninth. She should be in the tenth grade."

"She seems so smart. Was it any particular class she was struggling with?" Melinda asked carefully.

"Not really. Her grades started dropping after the divorce."

Ralph interjected, "That can affect a child, for sure."

"Yeah, and with me working all the time, I'm not home to help her very much with the homework or for that matter, to talk to her at all. She stays in her room most of the time."

"So sorry, Candi. I know it's been rough on you and her."

"Ahh, we'll make it. Just wish my loser ex-husband would throw some money our way every now and then to help with some of the expenses. He's about as sorry as they come."

No one really knew what to say, but hearing this gave Courtney a little more compassion for Lexi and the situation she was going through.

"Thanks, Mom. Great lunch."

"You're welcome, honey."

Courtney went to the guest room to find Lexi. Lexi was playing a game on her cell phone.

"Hey, Lexi?"

She didn't look up.

"I want you to know I really am sorry for being such a jerk earlier. I hope you can forgive me."

"As I said, earlier, whatever."

Courtney was hoping for a better response.

"Hey, you want to ride bikes? You could use mine and I'll use my old one."

Lexi hesitated, put the phone down, and finally looked up.

"Yeah, I'm pretty bored. I guess we could do that."

After Courtney cleared it with her parents and them telling the girls to be back for supper at 5:30, Courtney and Lexi went outside to the garage and got on the bikes.

"If you want, we can ride over to my best friend's house."

"Whatever."

When they got to Coco's house, they found her shooting some basketball. It wasn't that easy to dribble right-handed and shoot with the same hand. Her left arm in a sling was definitely an annoyance. They got off their bikes. Courtney was about to introduce Lexi when Lexi cut it short and asked Coco what happened to her arm.

"I fell on it a couple of days ago."

Lexi didn't show any signs of concern. Coco was holding the ball to her side and Lexi walked up to her, slapped the ball from her grip, and dribbled to the goal for a layup.

"I tell you what. Let's play you two against me. We'll play to twenty-one points. Make it, take it!"

Courtney asked what that meant. Lexi answered with disgust. "Seriously. You don't know what make it, take it means? It means whoever makes the shot gets the ball back in their possession. Understand?"

"Yeah, okay," Courtney answered, a little embarrassed.

"I'll let you two bring it in first," Lexi said.

The game began. Coco threw the ball to Courtney. She caught it and passed it back to Coco, who took a shot about ten feet away. The ball bounced off the hoop. Lexi rebounded it and shot. Nothing but net!

"Now that's how it's done, boys. Throw me the ball."

Courtney threw her the ball and she drove down toward the goal and easily passed Coco for a layup. This went on for about ten minutes, and the Courtneys didn't score a single point.

"You two are pathetic! Let's go riding," Lexi said.

The Courtneys looked despairingly at each other. "Let me ask my parents if it's okay," Coco said.

"Seriously?" Lexi asked. "How lame is that?"

Coco ignored the remark, went inside, and asked her Mom if it was okay for her to go bike riding with Courtney and her cousin. She told her it would be fine, not to stay out too late, and to take extra care of her left shoulder. Coco came out and noticed Lexi was already gone. "Where'd Lexi go?"

"She just took off and yelled at me for us to catch up with her. I don't know where she went," Courtney replied.

"Boy, she is really weird," Coco commented.

"That's putting it lightly," Courtney responded.

They rode off the driveway onto the road and caught a glimpse of Lexi, who was a good way ahead of them. They struggled but finally caught up with her, only because she had stopped.

"About time! What took you two slow pokes so long? Let's race. See the traffic light straight ahead? First one there wins. Go!"

All three of them took off. Of course, Lexi got there first.

"Man, you two are useless. A couple of losers," Lexi announced. "Hey, is there a convenience store nearby?" she asked.

"No, but there's a Dollar General ahead about three blocks from here," Courtney answered.

"Let's go there and get a drink," Lexi replied.

They got there and went inside. The Courtneys went straight to the cold drinks, but Lexi went walking through the store. They waited at the counter for Lexi and at last, she met them.

"Where's your drink, Lexi?" Courtney asked.

She answered, "I'm good. Let's get outta here."

The Courtneys paid for their Mountain Dews as Lexi walked out the door. They got back on their bikes and rode back to Coco's home. It was almost 5:30 and they needed to get to Courtney's home for dinner. The Courtneys said goodbye to each other. Lexi just rode away without saying anything. They arrived at Courtney's house. Lexi got off Courtney's bike, letting it fall to the ground.

"Hey, how about being a little nicer with my bike? You need to put it in the garage," Courtney yelled at her.

Lexi completely ignored her and went toward the back door of the house.

"You are such a jerk!" Courtney didn't know if Lexi heard her or not but didn't really care either way. Courtney put the bike she was riding in the garage and then went and picked hers up and put it in the garage too. Court's Mom noticed what seemed to be frustrating her daughter, and asked if everything was okay.

"Yes ma'am, it's fine."

Melinda then said to get cleaned up that supper would be ready in fifteen minutes. As Courtney walked by the guest room, she noticed Lexi pulling up her shirt and pulling something out of the waist of her pants. It looked like a shirt or jersey. She wondered if Lexi had stolen it from the Dollar General but if she had, wouldn't the alarm have sounded as she went out the front sliding glass doors? Seeing that, Courtney began to wonder if Lexi had taken her ring. She didn't know what to do. "Lord, I really need that wisdom I was asking You for earlier. Please, help me." She jumped in the shower, put on her pajamas, and then went to the kitchen to see if her Mom needed any help.

"I'm good. Thank you for asking, though. How about you help me clean up after dinner?"

"Sure, Mom. Hey, can I ask you something?"

"Of course. What is it?"

She told her Mom about the earlier events that had happened while they were out riding the bikes and told her the concerns she was having.

"Well, if she did take your ring and did steal something at the store, there would have to be proof before you make any accusations."

"Yeah, I know."

"I hope she's not doing any of this," Melinda said, "but when someone does steal, eventually they get caught."

At that time Candi, Lexi, and Ralph walked in and sat down for supper. Ralph said to Melinda, "Honey, this looks great! Thanks."

"You're welcome."

After the blessing, they all filled their plates with fried chicken, rice, English peas, and rolls.

After dinner and cleaning the dishes, they all went into the den and watched some mundane TV show. It was 10:00 pm. Ralph said he was going to bed and Melinda joined him. Before she walked out of the den, she said to Candi. "We both leave for work about 7:00 in the morning, so y'all are going to have to fend for yourselves for breakfast and lunch. I've got a roast cooking in the crock pot for supper. Courtney will be here if you have any questions."

Candi said they'd be fine. Courtney said she was going to bed, too. Candi and Lexi continued watching a 'Reba' rerun. When Courtney got into bed, she called Coco.

"What's up, girl?"

"I think Lexi stole something at the Dollar General today."

"What? Why do you think that?"

Courtney told her what she had seen.

"Well, you know, she didn't get a drink and it took her a while to get back to the front counter. Still, I hope you're wrong."

"I hope so too, Coco, but I don't think so. It wouldn't surprise me if she took my ring, too."

"What are you gonna do?" Coco asked.

"There's really nothing I can do until I find some concrete evidence to accuse her. I just wish my ring would show up."

Coco offered, "Hey, I'll come over tomorrow and we'll take a lot of time looking for it in your room. Maybe we'll find it."

"Sounds great. Call me tomorrow when you're headed this way," Courtney answered.

"Okay. Goodnight."

"Night."

Chapter Four: Rough Week

It was only Monday morning and already Courtney was tired of her relatives being at her house, mostly Lexi and her bad behavior. Courtney's parents had already left for work, and she didn't hear her Aunt or cousin. So, she assumed they were still asleep. She wished she didn't feel so uncomfortable around them, but she did, and nothing at this time helped her feel any different. Of course, she would continue to pray and ask the Lord to give her wisdom and strength to be a Christ-like witness to them. Her Mom had found some time to cook a few frozen sausage biscuits for them to eat. She was always so thoughtful. However, a big bowl of Cinnamon Crunch cereal sounded better to her. She got one of the biggest bowls, grabbed her Bible, and sat down to eat and read. Surprisingly, Lexi walked in. Courtney said good morning but got no reply. Lexi strolled over to the pantry and stared in it for a couple of minutes.

"This all you got?"

"Yeah. That's it, except for the sausage biscuits my Mom made before she left," Courtney responded with a slight attitude.

"She didn't make them. They're frozen, dip wad. All she did was throw them into the oven."

"More than you could probably do," Courtney said without thinking.

"I'm tired of your smart mouth. I might need to smack it into shape."

"Maybe you should quit calling me names."

"I call 'em as I see 'em," Lexi replied.

Courtney wanted to respond with another smart remark but chose not to. She knew it wasn't right for her to treat her cousin that way even though she was being a jerk. It sure was getting more and more difficult, though.

"What are you eating?" Lexi asked.

"Cinnamon Crunch."

"Where are the bowls?"

"In the third cabinet to your left." Lexi opened the cabinet door, snatched a bowl, seized the box of cereal from in front of Courtney, and poured it into her bowl.

"Got milk?"

Courtney so desperately wanted to make another smart-mouth remark like, "You have to get it from the cow in the backyard," but thought better of it.

"In the fridge. The spoons are in the drawer below the cabinet," Courtney added.

She whispered a prayer asking the Lord to help her attitude but wasn't feeling any better. "What are you reading?"

"The Bible."

"Oh yeah. I forgot. You're one of those crutch-needers."

Courtney quickly remarked somewhat sarcastically and held up her Bible, "Yeah, Lexi. You'd be right. I'm crippled with sin, and I need this crutch."

"You're a piece of work!" Lexi mocked.

"Yeah, you are..." Courtney stopped before she said something she'd regret.

"What were you saying?" Lexi snapped.

"Nothing."

"That's what I thought!"

After Lexi poured herself some milk into her bowl, she marched over to the TV, turned it on, and plopped down on the couch.

"Hey, Coco," Courtney answered her phone as she walked back to her bedroom, balancing her cereal in her other hand at the same time.

"Boy, you sound like a ray of sunshine this morning," Coco joked.

"I'm so tired of this situation. It is horrible!" Courtney snapped.

"Tell me about it, girl."

Courtney proceeded to tell her the details which had transpired during her breakfast.

"I'm so sorry, Court. I hate you're having to deal with this."

"Seriously, Coco. I don't know if I can make it without going off on her. I've come really close already."

"I wish I could do something to help," Coco said empathetically.

"Let's do something today so I can get out of here and away from the drama."

"Sounds good to me. Whatcha' wanna do?"

"Anything. Just so it's away from Lexi."

Coco wanted to remind Courtney that Jesus puts us into circumstances like this sometimes to make us depend on Him and make us stronger for other situations that are bound to come later. She held back thinking that Courtney probably wouldn't be very accepting of any spiritual encouragement at the moment.

"How about we ride our bikes to the playground and play some pickleball? They just got through constructing twelve new courts. I asked Mom and she even called your Mom and it's a go."

"Perfect! What time?" Courtney asked.

"Umm, say 11:00?" Coco answered.

"See ya there. Bring some money and we'll hit Tony's Pizzeria after we play."

"Awesome idea. Glad the struggle you've been going through hasn't caused your brain to go to mush," Coco chuckled.

"Yeah, well, between us two, someone has to have a brain."

"Ooh! Sassy too. See you at 11:00. Bye."

"Okay, bye."

Courtney was looking forward to getting away and spending time with her best friend. Pickleball and pizza! It was going to be a great day.

Courtney took off her pajamas and put on some shorts, a shirt, and her tennis shoes. She went out the door and went into the garage to get her pickleball paddle and balls. She grabbed the athletic bag and jumped onto her bike. It was 10:45 am and she couldn't wait to enjoy her day with Coco.

"Hey, where you going?" Lexi yelled out.

Courtney acted as if she didn't hear her. Lexi ran fast enough to stop her, grabbing the front handlebars of the bike.

"I asked you a question. Where you going?"

Dreadfully Courtney answered her. "I'm going to meet Coco at the playground to play some pickleball."

"Wait up. I'm gonna change into some other clothes. I'll go, too."

Inside Courtney's head, she was screaming. "No, no, no!" She couldn't believe that the awesome day she and Coco had planned had just crashed and burned. After ten anguishing minutes, Lexi came out, went to the garage, and jumped on the other bike.

"Lead the way," she said as bossy as ever.

Reluctantly, Courtney headed toward the playground.

Coco saw Lexi riding ahead of Courtney and could see the frustration and disappointment on Courtney's face.

"Let's go, Court?" Lexi yelled. "We gonna play some pickleball or what? Do they have any paddles here?"

"I think there are some plastic ones in the open cubbies over there. They're not the best, but they're still playable," Courtney responded woefully.

"Don't matter. I'm so good, I could play with tin foil paddles and still beat you two. In fact, we'll play one-on-two like we did in basketball. You two against me."

Courtney just rolled her eyes and walked on the court as if she were walking to death row. All the wind had been knocked out of her sail. She didn't even want to be there. Coco saw it written all over her face.

"Come on, Court. It'll be fun."

Courtney quietly said to Coco, "Yeah. As much fun as eating thumbtacks."

"I'll serve first." Lexi yelled.

Lexi served the ball to Coco and the ball whizzed right by her. Lexi hollered out a huge intimidating laugh. Then she served the pickleball to Courtney. Again, the ball whizzed right by her.

"Hey, how about slowing it down a little, Lexi? We're not pros."

"Okay, little ones. Ready Coco?"

She actually did slow the ball down enough for Coco to get a soft hit. It went back over the net so softly that it caught Lexi off guard and hit the ground twice before she could get to it. Lexi let out a couple of cuss words.

"Lexi, do me a favor and drop off the foul language," Courtney demanded.

"Why don't you make me?"

"Oh, that's real mature. I'm just asking you politely because there are children around and they don't need to be hearing words like that."

"Just serve the ball," Lexi demanded.

Coco served Lexi the ball and she hit it directly into Courtney's stomach. It stung a little, but Courtney didn't let it show.

"Alright, Ms. Sims, it's your turn to serve now. You think you can get it over the net?"

She ignored the remark and served the ball. Lexi teed off on it and it blew past both of them right down the middle.

"This is boring the he…, I mean, the heck out of me. Is that better Courtney?"

Lexi threw her paddle toward the cubbies, walked off the court, went to the swing set, and started swinging.

Coco said, "Try your best not to let her get to you. I know it's tough, but you can do it. Let's keep playing."

"I'm trying, Coco. Trust me. I'm trying," Courtney replied.

After about forty-five minutes, Lexi came back to the court.

"I've been watchin' you two play. You might as well give it up. You're not gonna get any better. You two ain't got any athletic skill. Losers! Let's go to Dollar General again. I need to get a few things."

"Hoping Lexi would get the hint," Courtney responded.

"No. We don't need anything. You can go by yourself."

"Well, are y'all gonna play pickleball all day or what?"

Before she knew it, Coco let it slip.

"We were gonna go to Tony's Pizzeria for lunch."

Courtney gave Coco a look that could kill. Coco mouthed she was sorry, that it just slipped out.

Lexi quickly answered, "Sounds good. We can go to the DG after that."

Before Courtney knew it, Lexi was getting on Courtney's bike. Courtney looked at Coco and sighed.

"Why can't she just leave?" Courtney asked sarcastically.

"I'm getting to see more and more why you're so irritated," Coco said while shaking her head back and forth annoyed. "She's definitely not the most enjoyable person to be around."

"Yeah, right?" Courtney replied with frustration.

Lexi then yelled out. "Come on, boneheads. I'm hungry. Where is this pizza place, anyway?"

The two Courtneys reluctantly slid onto their bikes and headed toward Tony's Pizzeria. It was one of the most favorite pizza restaurants in town. They had every type of pizza imaginable and many fantastic pasta dishes like their three-cheese spaghetti and meatballs, their double lasagna and their sausage filled ravioli.

The girls got there and Kevin was behind the counter. He was one of the senior high teenagers that went to their church. He'd been working there during the summer. When he saw the Courtneys he greeted them and introduced himself to Lexi. Lexi wasn't impressed enough with him, so she just ignored him. They found a table and sat down.

Coco said, "Mom gave me a coupon that we could use if you want. It's for a sixteen-inch, three-meat pizza for only $10.99. There are twelve slices on it, so we all could have four slices each."

"Perfect," Courtney replied.

Lexi countered in her usual manner. "I want just cheese. I don't like meat on my pizza. And might I add Coco, you must be a math wizard to have done that calculation so quickly in your head."

In a frustrated tone, Courtney quickly answered back, "You can just scrape off the meat on your four slices unless you have money to buy your own."

When Kevin came to their table to take their order Lexi jumped in and said, "We want a sixteen-inch pizza. We have a coupon for it, Kenny?"

"My name is Kevin."

Sarcastically, Lexi remarked, "Oh, I am so sorry for forgetting your name, Keith," She laughed out loud. "We want three whatever meats they want on one half and all cheese on the other half. Got it?"

The Courtneys were so caught off guard by Lexi's rudeness that they didn't say anything.

Kevin replied, "I'll have to ask the manager. Don't know if we can do that with this coupon."

"Seriously? Give me a break. If you can't do it, ask the owner to come talk to me."

"I'll be right back," Kevin said disgusted at Lexi's attitude.

Before he walked away Coco called him back. "Kevin, sorry to be such a problem. Why don't you just make the sixteen-inch three-meat pizza and make a small all-cheese pizza, too?"

"I can do that with no problem. And what three meats do you want? Pork sausage, pepperoni, and ham."

Coco looked at Courtney and asked her if she was fine with that, and she nodded yes.

"I'll bring you each a cup and you can go to the drinking fountain and get whatever you want. Pizzas should be out in about twenty minutes."

"Thanks, Kevin," Coco said.

Lexi got up and walked to the vintage pinball machine in the corner, put in fifty cents, and started playing the game.

"Why did you do that, Coco?" Courtney asked with agitation.

"I don't know. I just felt that it would be less conflict for everybody."

Courtney responded with the same irritation, "I'm so tired of her forcing her wants and intruding on what we want."

"Sorry. I just thought it would resolve the issue."

"I'm sorry, Coco. I don't mean to take it out on you. I'm just sick and tired of her snobby attitude, arrogance, and being such a jerk toward us."

"Can't really blame you, Court." Coco responded. "But you know as well as I do, our main purpose is to be a Godly influence on her."

"Yeah, I know, but I'm afraid this one might be too difficult to handle."

"Well, you'd be right with that thought. That's why we have to depend on the Lord to give us the strength."

"Easier said than done," Courtney replied with much skepticism.

In the corner, Lexi slapped the pinball machine and let out a couple of obscenities. The owner walked out into the dining area and asked.

"Is everything alright out here?" Lexi turned to him and answered.

"No! Your stupid machine over there is rigged. You owe me $1.50. It kept taking my money." The owner reached into his pocket and gave Lexi two dollars and apologized. When Lexi walked back to the table Courtney said, "You didn't put more than fifty cents into the pinball machine. Why did you lie?"

"Shut up!" Lexi whispered. "He might hear you. He's got plenty of money. You two need to know how to work the system if you're gonna get anywhere in this world."

Coco responded, "If that's working the system, I think I'll just stay stupid about it. I don't particularly care to rip people off."

"Ooh, little miss high and mighty. Excuse me. I didn't know you were so perfect. Oh, wait. You're one of those holy rollers like my cuz, aren't you?"

"If you mean a Christian, yeah. I'm definitely far from perfect, but I strive to put Christ first in my life and live it in His strength because I'm too weak to do it on my own. I have to depend on Him all the time."

"Well, I guess we're gonna have church here in a minute. Pass the offering plate. You two really bore me."

Kevin brought the two piping hot pizzas, three plates, napkins, and utensils over to their table. The pizzas smelled incredibly scrumptious. Lexi grabbed a slice of her all-cheese pizza and began eating it.

"I think I'll ask the Lord to bless this," Courtney offered.

She did and Lexi just kept on eating without any acknowledgement of their prayer of thanks. The Courtneys didn't say anything about it and dove into their sixteen-inch circle of fantasticness. They were never disappointed with Tony's pizzas. They were always the best and it was no disappointment this time either.

"This pizza sucks!" Lexi complained after eating three slices. "There's not enough cheese, the crust is too thick, and there's not enough tomato sauce either. Hey, Kenny."

Kevin walked to their table. "It's Kevin. Is there a problem?"

"Not really, that is if you like a cheese pizza with no cheese, no tomato sauce, and more crust than anything else."

Kevin knew better than to discuss the problem with someone like her who was just a chronic complainer. He reached for the pizza to get it replaced and she grabbed his hand.

"What are you doing?" Lexi asked incredulously.

"I'm taking this back and going to make you a new one."

"Never mind. Just give me my money back."

"You haven't paid any money, yet so I can make you another pizza or you can eat this one," Kevin firmly stated.

"You need to watch your attitude, boy! I wanna talk to the owner," Lexi demanded.

Kevin just rolled his eyes, turned around, and told the owner he was wanted by their little complainer. The owner came to their table and asked what the problem was. Lexi stated her complaint to him as he politely listened. After she was through, the owner remarked, "I apologize that you were disappointed with your pizza but there are only two options. We can make you another pizza or you can eat this one."

"Seriously? This place is bogus. Well, I sure ain't paying for it," Lexi smarted off.

Courtney had had enough and interjected herself into the conversation. "Sir, I'm sorry for the disturbance about all this. We'll be sure to pay for both pizzas. There won't be any more complaints. The pizzas are amazing as usual."

Lexi was outraged. "You're an idiot, and you, Mr. Owner, are an idiot and I'm leaving this place and telling everyone I meet that this place is pitiful."

"I'm sorry to hear that, ma'am, but we all have our opinions," the owner replied.

"Shut up, old man, and get outta my face."

"Lexi!" Courtney hollered.

Of course, Lexi ignored her and stomped out of the restaurant. Courtney apologized profusely to the owner for her cousin's actions.

"Sweetheart, don't you worry about it. The world is made up of all kinds, and I've seen them all."

He walked back to the kitchen. The Courtneys ate a couple more slices of their three-meat pizza. Kevin strolled over and chatted with them.

"Who was that girl?"

Reluctantly, Courtney answered, "I hate to admit it but it's my cousin. She and her Mom's house burned down, and they're staying with us this week."

"I'll be praying for you, girl. Whew! Haven't seen anyone act like that in quite a while."

"Yeah, me neither, Kevin. Sorry you were involved."

"No problem. Drama makes the day go by faster," he chuckled.

The Courtneys appreciated the levity.

"Thanks, Kev. Hey, can we get a to-go box?" Coco asked.

"Sure. I'll bring it and your check in a moment."

Well, the pizza ordeal was just another of the many difficult situations that had already happened since Lexi and her mother had come to stay at Courtney's house. She didn't know how much more she could handle. Hopefully, they would leave Friday as they had said they would. Lexi was outside the pizza restaurant standing by the bikes. She walked straight up to Courtney and got in her face.

"You ever embarrass me like that again and I will rip you a new one. Do you hear me?"

Courtney backed up away and said, "You can do whatever you want with me, but you acted horribly in there and I won't allow it."

"What? You won't allow it? Who do you think you are, you little twit?" With that, Lexi pushed Courtney to the ground and the leftover pizza she was holding went flying in the air, landing all over the sidewalk. Coco jumped in front of Lexi, grabbed her, and told her to stop. Lexi, stronger than both of them, shoved Coco down. She landed on her left shoulder. It was excruciating. Not only that, but Lexi pushed her into one of the nearby bikes. The sharp edges of one of the pedals caused a deep gash in her right leg and it was bleeding very badly. Courtney jumped up and ran as hard as she could and knocked Lexi to the ground. Then she pounced on her and started hitting her over and over with her fists. Lexi was able to maneuver out from under her and started wailing at Courtney. That's when the owner of Toni's Pizzeria came out. He grabbed Lexi and told them all to stop. Lexi jerked away and told him to let her go. He released his grip on Lexi and knelt down to check on the damage to Coco's leg.

"Stay here. I'll get you some antiseptic and a Band-Aid. Is your arm, okay?"

"Yessir. Just aches a little from falling on it."

"Okay. I'll be right back."

Lexi didn't show any sympathy and jumped on her bike and rode away.

The Courtneys, sitting across from each other on the pavement, just stared at each other for a minute.

"You, okay?" Courtney asked her best friend.

"Yeah. I'll be fine. The gash has stopped bleeding now. What just happened here?" Coco asked, still confused.

"I think we fell into 'Lexi Zone.'" Courtney responded. "She does that to you."

"Yeah, it would seem," Coco replied.

The owner came back outside and started applying some ointment he had for Coco's leg. He then placed a Band-Aid on it.

"I know it hurts but I think you'll be fine. That kid, referring to Lexi, has some serious discipline problems."

"That's for sure," Courtney said.

"Is she a friend of y'all?"

"She's actually my cousin, but you're exactly right. She definitely needs some correction in her life. Again, I'm so sorry for all the disturbance."

"I appreciate the apology but as I told you inside, I've seen all kinds. I just hope your cousin makes some changes before it's too late. By the way, I'm cooking you two another pizza since that one got spattered all over the sidewalk."

"That is so kind of you," Coco said, "But that's not necessary and we don't have any more money to pay for it."

"It's on the house."

Both Courtneys told him thanks and that they would be sure to clean up the pizza on the sidewalk. He told them thank you and would see them next time. As he walked back inside, they started cleaning up the mess on the sidewalk. A few minutes later, Kevin walked out and gave them their pizza.

"Hope the rest of your day goes well. I'll see y'all Sunday."

They both said thanks and goodbye.

"Well, another great episode in the lives of Courtney's relatives," Courtney exclaimed with frustration. "I don't know what I'm gonna do when I see her at my house."

"Whew! That will be tough. This is one of those times I wish the Lord would give us a magic wand to make everything better."

"Yeah, that would be nice," Courtney sighed.

"I know you probably don't feel like it at this moment, but we need to pray and ask the Lord how to handle this."

"You're right about one thing, I sure don't feel like praying, but you're right. You mind doing the praying?" Courtney asked.

They bowed their heads and Coco asked God to give them wisdom, compassion, and strength to deal with Lexi, her Mom, and whatever other situations might happen while they are staying with Courtney's family.

"Thanks, Coco. I guess we better be getting back home, but first, I'm eating a couple of slices of this hot pizza."

"Now that sounds like a plan!" Coco said with a big smile.

After scarfing down a couple of slices between them, they got on their bikes and went to Courtney's house. Courtney was able to maneuver carrying the pizza and ride her bike as they headed to her house. When they walked in, they saw Lexi sitting in front of the TV on the couch with her Mom. Her Mom was drinking a beer and by the sight of the table in front of them, it looked like she'd already downed two others.

"Well, what are you two hoodlums doing? Yum, pizza. Gimme a slice."

Courtney gave her Aunt the box, and she grabbed a slice and asked Lexi if she wanted one.

"Sure."

"I didn't think you like meat on your pizza," Courtney inquired.

"What's it to you, looser?"

"Now Lexi, that's no way to talk to your cousin. Be nice."

Lexi completely ignored her mother's light scolding and ate her slice of pizza.

"Lexi told me that you all left her at the Dollar General today. Why did you all do that?"

Courtney answered, "Because we didn't leave her. In fact, we didn't even go to the Dollar General. She actually was the one who left us. I guess she didn't tell you what happened at the pizza place."

Lexi jumped in quickly and with a menacing look on her face. "Nothing happened there other than me playing a lame pinball machine, and you two flirting with that Kevin kid."

Courtney was about to speak when Coco interrupted and said to Lexi and her Mom, "Yeah, that was about all. Courtney and I stayed a little longer at Toni's. I guess that's when you left to go to the store."

"Yeah, that's right. I guess I forgot you two didn't go with me," Lexi agreed.

"Well, Lexi, you should be more careful accusing others when you have the facts mixed up."

"Yeah, whatever," Lexi replied disrespectfully.

Her Mom downed the remaining contents of her beer and told the girls that she was going to lie down for a while.

That was the queue for the Courtneys to leave and go to Courtney's bedroom.

"Why did you back Lexi's story up? We could have nailed her," Courtney asked Coco with aggravation.

"I'm sorry, but I thought it was best. If we had told her Mom the whole story, she wouldn't have done anything anyway. Lexi would have just gotten mad and would eventually take it out on you."

"Gosh! She makes me so mad. I just want her and her Mom to leave. I'm so sick of them."

Coco, trying to respond with empathy said, "I get it, Court. I'm so sorry you're having to deal with this. Hey, I've got an idea. Why don't I ask my parents if it would be okay for you to spend the rest of the week at our house?"

"Great idea! You think they'd do it?" Courtney asked.

"Why not? We've done it before when your parents have been out of town," Coco answered.

"Yeah, but what reason would we give them?"

"Hmm. How about that it was getting a little crowded with Lexi and her Mom here?"

"Yeah, that might work." After Courtney hesitated, she looked frustrated and said, "My parents aren't going to go for it. They're probably gonna tell me that it would be rude to leave Lexi here by herself."

"Just ask. It can't hurt. I'll check with my parents first to make sure it's okay with them."

Coco called her Dad, and he said if it were okay with her Mom then it would be fine. Her Mom said it was fine as long as Courtney's parents were okay with it.

"Okay, we're halfway home. Call your parents and tell them that we invited you over for a few days."

"Okay. Here goes nothing."

Courtney phoned her Mom's cell phone because she knew that her Dad would just tell her to call her Mom and get her okay. Melinda answered her cell.

"Hey, sweet. What do you need? I'm about to go into a meeting here at work."

"Umm, Coco asked me if I could spend a few days at her house. I thought it might help with things being so crowded here. Would that be, okay?"

Immediately Melinda gently responded, "Absolutely not! You have your cousin here who you should be entertaining and getting to know."

"But Mom."

"No buts. I've gotta go. I'll see you when I get home."

Courtney looked at Coco and groaned. "Told ya. I knew it was a hopeless idea."

Right at that moment Lexi busted into the bedroom.

"It's a good thing you two didn't say anything about our little altercation at the pizza place. I would've hated to teach you two a lesson."

Courtney looked straight into Lexis' face and said, "Why are you so mean, Lexi? Why do you treat people so badly?"

"I guess you're going to play Dr. Phil now, and tell me that life is much better when you're kind and considerate to others? You two have no clue about life. You're only twelve and your little lives are perfect. You both have a Mom and a Dad who give you whatever you want. You have nice houses that haven't burned down with all your stuff in them. Life stinks! No one can tell me otherwise. So, shut your mouth and make sure you don't cause me any problems."

With that, she stomped out. Neither Courtneys knew what to say. They hadn't really given much thought to Lexi's situation and what she'd gone through. She was actually correct. The best friends had it really nice, and maybe even forgot just how good their lives were. Hearing Lexi made them really stop and think.

"I hate to admit it, but Lexi is right," Coco stated.

Courtney slowly looked up from the floor and stared at her best friend and said, "Yeah, I guess so. But it doesn't make it right how she's treating me and you and everyone else."

"You're right, but it does remind us that we need to treat her the way we would want to be treated."

"The Golden Rule, huh?"

"Yeah," Coco answered.

"So how do we do that?"

"I don't know. I just know, just like you do, that it's the right thing to do."

"Another prayer moment?"

"Yeah, and you pray this time," Coco told Courtney.

She did and asked the Lord to show them how to respond and do the right thing with Lexi.

"I better be getting home. Talk to you later tonight."

"Okay," Courtney responded. "Talk to ya later."

Later that evening Coco was in her bedroom and decided to call Courtney.

"You asleep?"

"Nah, just reading a couple of chapters in a novel."

"Cool! I have an idea. Why don't we ask our parents if we can go skating tomorrow? We'll ask Lexi if she wants to go, too."

"Why ask her? She'd just make it another horrible experience."

"Probably, but we gotta start somewhere. My Mom and Dad said it would be fine. In fact, Mom said it would even be okay to ride my bike if we wanted to."

Unenthusiastically Courtney responded, "I'll be honest. I'm not looking forward to the idea of inviting Lexi, but I'll ask my parents and if they say it's okay then I'll ask Lexi."

"Let me know what you find out," Coco said.

Within a few minutes, the plans had been made. They were all set to ride their bikes and go skating the next day at 11:00. When Lexi was asked if she wanted to go with them, she groaned out an answer saying that she would go and be their babysitter. Her mother told her that was uncalled for. Lexi just brushed off the comment.

"I'll be bored whether I go with you losers or stay here."

Courtney was quick to answer, "Don't feel that you have to."

Hoping she would change her mind, but to Courtney's disappointment, she didn't. Courtney prayed for compassion for Lexi but truthfully, it was very difficult to have any. She texted Coco to tell her it was a go, and that Lexi did decide to go, too. It was just a minute or two before she received a text from Coco that she was praying that tomorrow could be a breakthrough in the situation.

Chapter Five: No Lexi, For Now

Tuesday morning came early but it was going to be a much better day. It was going to be a Lexi-less day. Courtney's Mom told her that her Aunt and Lexi had to go back to Tupelo to meet with the insurance adjuster about their house and belongings, but they would be back later that evening since they didn't have anywhere to stay. Also, she told Courtney to wait till Wednesday to go skating so Lexi wouldn't miss out. Court was hoping that she and Coco could go skating today without Lexi, but that hope was blown away. Anyway, it was such a relief knowing that she wouldn't have to deal with Lexi and her antics today. Courtney called Coco and told her the great news. They both were disappointed about not going skating and decided to get together later that morning and determine what their day would consist of. Courtney rode her bike to Coco's home. Vicki, Coco's Mom, greeted her and asked if she wanted one of the cinnamon rolls, she had baked earlier that morning.

"Absolutely. Thanks, Ms. Lawrence."

"You're very welcome, Courtney."

Coco heard her from her room and told her to come to her room. Courtney tried to answer her, but her mouth was filled with a ton of deliciousness.

"Okay. Coco began. What are our plans?"

"We haven't been bowling all summer. What do you say we do that?" Courtney replied while wiping her mouth.

"Now that sounds great," Coco replied. "In fact, Susan at church was telling me that they had a summer special. Three games, shoes, a burger, fries, and a drink, all for $10.00."

Courtney said, "You might have to spot me the $10. I didn't bring any money."

"No problem. Call your Mom and I'll check with mine." Both parents said their plans would be fine. Vicki asked them if they wanted her to drive them there. The girls said thanks and told her they would just ride their bikes if it was okay. She assured them it was and told them to be careful.

"What about money? What does bowling cost these days?"

Coco told her Mom about the summer special. Vicki gave them a twenty-dollar bill and told them to enjoy their selves. Both hugged her and were off.

They got to the bowling alley at about 11:30. They saw a few of their friends from church, and they called for them to join them. The Courtneys said they'd get their shoes and balls and would be right there. After three hours of bowling, being with friends, and eating a tasty burger and fries, they were ready to head back to their homes. On their way back, Coco asked Courtney if she wanted to spend the night with her.

"I'll ask Mom when we get to the house." As soon as they walked in, Courtney asked her Mom if it would be okay to spend the night with Coco.

Her Mom said, "Sure," but then remembered. "Oh, I forgot, honey. Your Aunt and cousin will be back tonight from Tupelo, and it would be good for you to be here."

"Why, Mom?" Courtney asked with disappointment.

"It just would, Court. They are our relatives, and we need to be here for them."

"But, Mom."

"Court, I'm sorry but not tonight."

She dropped her head and walked Coco out the backdoor. "Today was so awesome, but now I have to endure the Lexi crud again."

"So sorry, Court. Maybe their road trip will make things better."

"I doubt it, Coco."

They told each other goodbye, and Coco rode back to her house.

Courtney wanted to go to bed but her parents wanted her to stay up with them until her Aunt and cousin got home. Candi and Lexi pulled into the Sim's driveway at about 9:30 pm. When they walked in the front door, Lexi shot straight to the guestroom.

"Lexi, you can at least say hello."

"Hello," Lexi replied in a low tone as she continued walking.

"I'm sorry, y'all. She seems to be taking this much harder than I thought she would," Candi apologized.

"That's perfectly understandable. You and Lexi have been uprooted from your home and your normal routine. Anyone would struggle with that. We're glad you two got there and back safely. How did the insurance meeting go?" Melinda asked.

"As expected, it seems we'll be able to get a full replacement for the trailer. The only problem is that the policy didn't have much in the contents section. It doesn't hardly cover the furniture much less our clothes, dishes, jewelry, appliances, and the other necessities."

"Oh no, sis. I'm so sorry."

"Thanks, but we'll be alright. I'm bushed. If you don't mind, I think I'm going to head to bed."

"Absolutely, sis," Melinda replied. "I'll get up a little earlier tomorrow before going to work and make you all a hearty breakfast."

"Please don't put yourself out, Mel. We can eat some cereal or something."

"Let me do this for you two. I want to."

They hugged each other and all went to bed. Candi turned back around and asked Melinda if she could talk to her for a moment. She said sure.

Chapter Six: Lexi's Back In Full Throttle

Wednesday morning, Courtney woke up hungry and decided to cook herself some breakfast. Her parents had already left to go to work and as promised, her Mom had cooked an amazing breakfast- eggs, biscuits, bacon, and even pancakes. She also left a note saying to have a great day at the skating rink and to tell Coco to be extra careful with her shoulder. She had left some money to cover hers, Coco's, and Lexi's skate cost. Courtney spooned two scrambled-to-perfection eggs out of the covered pan, lathered more butter than she should have on two biscuits, and grabbed three crispy strips of bacon and two fluffy pancakes. She couldn't wait to dig into it, but before eating, she wanted to text her Mom and tell her thanks. She walked back to her room to get her phone but when she walked back in, Lexi was seated at the table eating what Courtney had fixed.

"Hope you're enjoying my breakfast!" Courtney said with disdain.

"Yep, sure am. Pretty good, too. I would have scrambled the eggs slightly less, but they'll do. I also like my bacon a little less crispy. Hope the pancakes are okay."

Courtney was fuming inside. "No one is forcing you to eat any of it."

Lexi just kept on chewing and totally ignored Courtney's statement. It took everything within Courtney to not say something nasty to Lexi. She quietly got a spoonful of eggs and got a biscuit, some bacon, and a couple of pancakes even though she didn't have much of an appetite now. Within minutes, she was enjoying her second-made breakfast in her bedroom. She had to get away from her cousin.

A few minutes later, Lexi opened Courtney's bedroom door and asked, "What time are we leaving for the rink?"

Courtney finished her bite of food and answered without looking at her, "At about 10:45."

"I ain't riding that stupid little bike. I'm riding yours," Lexi commented.

Before Courtney could respond, it was too late. Lexi had already shut the door. She thought about calling her Mom and telling her about all that had been happening. She had had enough. She picked up her phone and saw Coco's name flash across the screen.

"What's going on, girl? We're gonna have so much fun today."

"Don't think so," Courtney said with hopelessness.

"Oh, no. Lexi again?"

"Of course."

Coco asked her what the problem was this time. Courtney proceeded to tell her about the morning events.

"Court, this is horrible, but I gotta tell you. You handled this morning like a pro, or maybe I should say like Jesus," Coco said trying to console Courtney.

"Well, thanks for the compliment, but I'm sure not feeling like Jesus. I'm so angry inside I just wanna scream."

"Totally understandable. Tell you what. When we get to the skating rink, you and I will go outside, and you can scream to your content as long and as loud as you want. I might even join you."

They both chuckled a little.

"I'll see you here around 10:45."

"Okay."

Courtney decided not to call her Mom and to manage the situation with the Lord's strength and wisdom and her best friend's help. When Courtney came out of her room, her Aunt Candi had just finished eating and was washing the dishes and cleaning up.

"Oh, I'm sorry Aunt Candi. Let me do this."

"Oh thanks, Court, but I'm almost through. It's no big deal."

Courtney thanked her and told Lexi that Coco was on her way. She didn't look up from whatever she was doing on her cell and just grunted.

"So, what are y'all plans today, girls?"

Of course, Lexi didn't answer. So, Courtney did.

"We are going skating. Coco is coming over now, and we'll be leaving as soon as she gets here."

"How much does it cost?"

"Only ten bucks each but don't worry about it. Mom paid for all three of us."

"Well, that was super nice. I've gotta great sis and you've gotta great Mom, that's for sure."

Lexi was on the couch sticking her finger into her mouth faking a gag reflex as if to say, "Y'all are making me sick."

Coco arrived right on time. They all got on their bikes and took off to the skating rink. As they rode, Lexi, in her own annoying way, every now and then, would sway into the path of one of the Courtneys, causing them to maneuver their bikes so they wouldn't crash. One time, Courtney almost hit a tree off the sidewalk. She yelled at Lexi to stop it and, of course, Lexi just yelled back, "You wanna make me?"

Courtney ignored it and they just kept enough distance from Lexi so she couldn't cause any more trouble. Thankfully, they finally reached the skating rink and paid to go inside. The Courtneys went one way and Lexi went her way once they all got their skates.

"I'm so glad she didn't stay with us. I can't wait till they leave," Courtney said.

"Have you heard when Lexi and her Mom are leaving?" Coco asked.

"No. I hope it's sooner than later. Let's skate."

Lexi hadn't been on the skating rink floor for no more than ten minutes when the manager already called her down for skating so recklessly. She just gave her a look like she could care less. As soon as the Courtneys started skating, Lexi zipped over and almost hit them, causing Coco to almost fall down. Lexi stopped directly in front of them.

"Let's race."

They both declined. Lexi called them chicken and sped away in disgust. After about forty-five minutes, the Courtneys decided to rest for a moment. They were on the sidelines when they saw Lexi knock a small girl onto the railing. One of the other skaters helped the child up. She was okay, just a little rattled. The manager had been keeping an eye on Lexi and whistled her to come to her. Lexi skated over showing her disrespect.

"What do you want?"

"I've called you down one time already. This is the second time. There won't be any other warnings. Next time you'll be leaving the premises. Do you understand?"

Lexi responded, "Whatever!" and skated off.

The Courtneys strolled back onto the floor and started skating again. Swoosh! Lexi came zooming by and almost knocked the Courtneys off their balance again. She turned to look at any hopeful devastation she'd left behind and when she did, she accidentally ran into another teenage girl about the same age. They both fell on top of each other. Lexi got up first and started yelling at the girl.

"You are so stupid. Don't you know how to skate?"

The girl did not back down and replied, "What? You ran into me, you idiot."

That was all it took. Lexi rolled straight to the girl and knocked her down. The girl got up and grabbed Lexi by her shirt and pulled her down on the hard surface. Lexi, surprised by the girl's response, got up and grabbed her. They both started wrestling with each other. The manager and the maintenance supervisor ran over to where they were and separated them.

"Out! Both of you. Now!" The manager shouted.

The teenage girl tried to plead her case saying it wasn't her fault and that Lexi had started it, but to no avail. The manager put them both out. As Lexi was taking off her skates, she yelled at the Courtneys to come there, "We're leaving."

They told her they weren't leaving. Looking at Courtney, Lexi pulled a dirty trick.

"Fine! I'll just make sure your Mom knows that you caused all this mess."

"She won't believe you. I'll just have her call the manager and she'll tell her what really happened."

At that moment, the manager came over and asked the Courtneys if Lexi was with them. They told her yes.

"I'm sorry then, but I'm going to have to ask you two to leave, as well."

"Why?" Coco asked politely.

"It's just best. I don't need any additional problems."

"But we would never do anything like that. You've seen us here before," Courtney commented.

"Yes, I have and you two have never been any problem, but I've had a couple of parents who are worried that more of this will happen since you are associated with that one," she said, pointing to Lexi. The Courtneys couldn't believe it. Another potential fun event was totally ruined because of Lexi. They took their skates off and went outside where Lexi was waiting for them.

"About time. Let's go to the Dollar General."

"No," Courtney abruptly said.

"Let me put it this way. We're going or I'm going to tell your parents that you cussed the manager out when you left."

"She won't believe you."

"Who knows? I can be very convincing."

"You really are a jerk, Lexi."

"Watch out, little Christian. You shouldn't be calling me names, now, should you?" Lexi replied mockingly.

Courtney kept the responses to herself that she wanted to say and looked at Coco. They agreed to go to the store.

They all walked in, Lexi, as usual, went her own way. The Courtneys grabbed a pack of cheese crackers and a soft drink and ambled to the counter and paid for them. They saw Lexi heading for the door and when she went through the entrance a security alarm went off. The lady behind the counter told Lexi to stop. Vintage Lexi, she didn't. She jumped on her bike and took off. Ironically, a policeman had just pulled into the parking lot and watched the whole scene. The lady employee yelled at the policeman, while pointing toward Lexi and told him that girl on the bike had just stolen something from the store. The policeman pulled out of his parking spot and drove after her. With his siren screaming, he caught up with her in seconds, pulled in front of her, and told her to stop.

"What are you stopping me for? I ain't done nothing," Lexi spurted.

"The store clerk said the alarm went off when you went through it. I'll need you to ride your bike back to the store so we can settle this issue."

With a disgusted look, Lexi turned her bike around and rode back to the store. She got off and the policeman walked beside her into the store.

"What did you take?" The store clerk asked Lexi.

"Nothin'!"

"Well, the alarm doesn't just go off by itself."

"Did you hear it when I came in just now? Nope! You didn't because I didn't take nothin'."

The policeman promptly told her to empty her pockets.

"Really?" Lexi smarted off. Shaking her head in disgust, she emptied her front and back pockets. They were completely empty.

"Satisfied?" Lexi said staring straight at the employee and officer.

"Alright. I can't see any reason to continue detaining you," the officer told Lexi.

"I ain't ever coming back to this store again and I'm tellin' everybody I know that they shouldn't ever shop here. I should sue this dump! And you need to get your stupid alarm fixed!" She stomped out of the store.

The Courtneys got on their bikes and noticed Lexi had stopped a few yards ahead of them and gotten off her bike. She was picking up something from the ditch. When they rode closer to her, they saw her pick up what looked like brand-new sunglasses. Lexi noticed them and put them on.

"Yo! Ain't I the lucky one? Can't believe I found these in the ditch."

"Lexi, you need to take them back to the store, now," Courtney said sternly.

"Take what back. I just found these. Why would I take them to that store?"

"We know you stole them, Lexi. We're not stupid!" Courtney countered.

"Well, that statement that you two aren't stupid can be discussed for another day, but I don't like you accusing me of stealing these sunglasses. You need to keep your mouths shut or I'll shut it for you."

"You know, Lexi. Eventually, you're going to get into some big trouble. You're really playing with fire," Coco interjected.

"Shut up, bozo. You don't even know what you're talking about."

At that, Lexi rode off toward Courtney's home.

"I gotta tell my parents and her Mom about this," Courtney said to Coco.

"Maybe so, Court, but I'm not sure what good it's going to do at this point. If her Mom confronts her, it'll be our word against hers and most likely just cause more grief."

Courtney kicked an empty dog food can that was in the ditch as hard as she could.

"She's so bad and mean! She gets away with everything."

"I know it seems that way now, but sooner or later, she's gonna get caught or worse, maybe even injured, if she doesn't stop her horrible actions. She's just deceiving herself that this type of living will bring her happiness. I just wished we could think of something that would get through to her."

"Yeah, I guess. Well, we better get back. We've got youth Bible study tonight."

"Oh yeah!" Courtney exclaimed. "I can't wait. At least Lexi won't be there."

"Don't you think we should invite her?" Coco asked.

Courtney just stared at Coco for a few seconds, "Seriously? But I don't want her there."

"I know Court. Me either, to be honest, but you know we have got to do whatever we can to help her. Just maybe she'll come, hear Steve's lesson, meet some of our friends, and really enjoy it."

"Yeah. You're probably right now that I think about it. In fact, I just saw an elephant go into the front door of the Dollar General." Coco actually turned to look and then realized that Courtney was making a smart remark.

"You got me, Court, but you know there's always the possibility that God would use tonight to reach her. God can do anything."

"Okay, okay. I'll ask her to go."

Then she let out a soft scream of frustration, "Ahh!"

Since the Courtneys lived just a couple of blocks away from each other, they separated a block away and went to their own homes. When Courtney walked into their home, she heard Lexi and her Mom screaming at each other. Courtney saw her Mom and Dad standing in the kitchen listening. She asked them what was going on and her Mom told her that Candi decided to go to church tonight and told Lexi she was going, too. Lexi had been arguing with her for the last twenty minutes about not going.

"Why did Candi want to go?"

"I'm not sure but she and I had a long hard talk last night before we went to bed. She broke down and admitted that she knew some things had to change in her life. She even told me that she used to think she was a Christian but now she wasn't sure. She said all the junk that she'd been experiencing over the last few years had really gotten her down. I think the Lord is truly beginning to deal with her."

"That would be awesome and even more so if Lexi would change," Ralph added.

"Don't expect it to happen," Courtney said.

Both parents gave her a stern look. Her Dad asked her why she would say that so emphatically.

"Sorry, Dad, but you haven't been around her this week like I have. She's just not a nice person and that's putting it mildly."

Her Dad responded, "Well, you know as well as your Mom and me that the Lord can change anyone."

"Yessir," she answered, still not believing it could happen to Lexi. She told the Lord she was sorry for thinking that and to help her with that unbelief and to pray for her even more.

Chapter Seven: Church! No Way

At that moment, they heard Lexi yell out that she wasn't going to church. She then slammed the guestroom door where she and her Mom had been arguing. She threw the door open and stomped past Courtney and her parents, straight out the back door. Melinda went into the bedroom and found her sister lying on the bed crying uncontrollably. Melinda put her arms around her and tried her best to console her. Ralph asked Courtney to go with him outside and to try to calm Lexi. When they went outside, they caught a glimpse of her riding away on Courtney's bike. They both yelled for her to come back, but she continued to ride. "Get lost!" she hollered.

"Should we go after her, Dad?"

"Maybe it'd be best to let her be by herself for a few minutes to try and cool down."

They went back inside and found Melinda in the kitchen. Candi was beside her drinking some water. Candi had calmed down a little but was visibly upset and apologized to them over and over for the disturbance. They told her not to worry about it, and that they understood.

"Is Lexi outside?" Candi asked Ralph and Courtney.

"No, but we saw her ride away on Courtney's bike. Maybe she just needs a little time to cool down," Ralph said, giving his fatherly opinion.

"She's out of control. I don't know what to do."

Melinda put her arm around her sister again. "She probably needs some time alone."

"Y'all need to be going to church," Candi commented. "I'm going to stay here and wait for Lexi to come back. Hopefully, she'll be back soon."

"No, we'll stay here with you. We don't have to go."

"Please, Melinda. I'd feel horrible if you didn't go just because of this."

"You sure you'll be alright?"

"I'll be fine."

"Okay, but if you need us, I'll have my cell with me at church."

"Thanks, sis."

Courtney and her parents left a few minutes later and went to the evening services at their church. On their way, Ralph said they should pray for them. Courtney and her Mom closed their eyes and Ralph prayed.

"Lord, we thank You for who You are and what You mean to our family. We come to You on behalf of Candi and Lexi. Please bring them to You. Help us to be there for them during these difficult times. We love You, Jesus. Amen."

They arrived at the church shortly after the prayer and were too late for the Wednesday night supper. The kitchen help had just finished cleaning up everything. Courtney's parents went into the sanctuary and sat down next to Coco's parents. Courtney went into the Christian Life Center where the teens met each Wednesday evening. Coco saw her and ran over to her.

"Hey, girl. Why are you so late?"

"Another ordeal in the Lexi saga," Courtney replied.

"Give me the run down?"

"When I got home, Lexi and her Mom were having a fight. Lexi's Mom told her they were going to church, and Lexi went ballistic. She told her Mom she wasn't going and ran out of the house, jumped on my bike, and took off."

"Whoa! She's seriously out of control."

"That's exactly what Aunt Candi said about her."

"I think it's pretty cool, though, that your Aunt was going to come tonight."

"Yeah. Mom said that they have had a couple of talks lately. Mom thinks the Lord is really dealing with her."

"Oh, I hope so. I wish He would do that with Lexi."

Steve, the student minister called out, "Alright, everybody. Grab a seat and let's have our Bible study."

It took only a few minutes for them to finally settle down.

"So glad you all are here tonight. I wanted to talk to you about something that's been a struggle for me throughout my Christian walk. Loving people who are just plain unlovable."

The Courtneys both turned and looked at each other simultaneously with a look of amazement on each other's faces. They couldn't believe that Steve was going to speak on this subject. They leaned in because they wanted to hear what he had to say since they had been struggling with the Lexi situation.

"When I was at my last church, there was a gentleman that was always in a bad mood, and he had this uncanny ability to make everyone else in a bad mood. It didn't matter what we were discussing, he seemed to be against it. It didn't make a difference what event we were considering to have, he opposed it. I tried my best to be a friend, but he was one of these people who always had to be right, constantly upped you in a discussion, and never was agreeable on anything."

Coco raised her hand.

"Yeah, Coco," Steve questioned.

"Do you know what caused him to be that way?"

"I never found out. In fact, I was on staff at that church for five years and never heard why he had such a bad disposition and was so disagreeable. I even went to him and asked him if I had offended him in some way and if I had, I was truly sorry. He didn't say a word to me. He just stared at me like I was an alien and walked away."

One of the teenage boys interrupted and asked, "I know a guy at school who's kinda like that. Nobody wants to be around him because he's such a jerk to everyone."

You could hear a low rumbling in the room because people were talking about individuals, they knew who were just like that. Of course, the Courtneys had the same person in mind-Lexi.

Steve got control of the group discussion and continued. "By listening to all the chatter, it seems like we all know individuals like that. I would love to tell you that he changed and ended up being one of the strongest servants of the Lord and the nicest person in the church, but sadly enough, as far as I know, he has never changed. It truly bothered me, and I searched the scriptures to find an answer. The Lord showed me a passage that gave me a little insight and perhaps it will be an encouragement to you with that individual you are grappling with. Oh, let me change that. It might give you direction in handling that situation because, to be honest, it's not that encouraging."

Steve gave a slight chuckle.

"It's found in Luke 6:27-28. *But I say to you who hear, love your enemies, do good to those who hate you, bless those who curse you, pray for those who mistreat you.*' When I read that verse, I was like you're kidding, right Lord? Why couldn't it have said, "But I say to you who hear, you don't have to love your enemies and the unlovable?"'" Everyone laughed. "Seriously. Wouldn't it be so much easier if we could just discount those kinds of people and forget them? But we can't. The Lord told us that it doesn't matter how we're treated by them, or how they respond to our kindness and generosity. We are supposed to continue loving them and treating them with kindness."

Another one of the older students interrupted. "Wait a minute, Steve. If I have a person that is really horrible to me and everyone around her, I'm supposed to act like she's great?"

"Good question. Let me explain what I believe about that. Jesus didn't command us to like them but to love them. Even Jesus couldn't force the ones who hated Him and treated Him so badly, to love Him, but he did treat them with love and respect. The way I understand this concept is this- Real love is shown toward a person when they are in need. You and I should always be willing to help them when they are in trouble or in need. You don't have to like them or the way they treat you, but you do have to love them. Make sense everyone?"

All the students seemed to grasp the lesson but knew it was a challenge.

"Cool. If you need to talk to me about someone or a situation that you're battling with in regard to this lesson tonight, I'll be glad to pray with you and help you through it. Alright, who's ready for some volleyball?"

The students broke into teams and enjoyed a great evening of fellowship and fun. At about 8:00, everyone was leaving the church to go home. The Courtneys and their parents said goodbye and said that they would be praying for Melinda's sister and niece.

Courtney and her parents walked into their home and saw Candi completely in a panic.

"Candi, what's wrong?" Melinda curiously asked.

"Lexi hasn't come home."

"She's been gone ever since she left the house?" Ralph inquired.

"Yes. I haven't heard from her at all. I drove around your neighborhood but never saw her."

"Courtney, would you have any idea where she would have gone?"

"No sir," She replied.

"Okay. Melinda, you and Candi stay here and keep your phones nearby. Courtney and I are going to drive around and see if we can spot her anywhere."

All agreed with the plan. In the car, Ralph asked Courtney again if she could think of any place she might be.

"The playground might be a good place to start. She also likes going to the Dollar General but..." She didn't finish her statement. Dad noticed with curiosity and asked her why she stopped midsentence.

"What's that all about, Courtney? Why did you stop after mentioning the Dollar General?"

"Umm, well, there was a little incident that happened yesterday when we were there, and I didn't want to mention it because it would have gotten Lexi in trouble."

"What happened, sweet?"

"The store clerk accused her of stealing something because the alarm at the entrance went off when she walked through it. She yelled at Lexi to stop but she quickly rode away. There happened to be a police officer that was getting out of his car in the Dollar General parking lot. When the clerk saw him, she told him what had happened. He got back in his car and drove up the road, caught up with Lexi, and made her ride back to the store."

"Did she steal something?"

"Well, the policeman talked to her and asked her to empty her pockets but she didn't have anything. He let her go and she left the store screaming that she could sue them for falsely accusing her. Coco and I left a minute or so after Lexi, and we saw her grabbing sunglasses in the ditch. She claimed that she had just found them, but we think she threw them in the ditch before the officer caught up with her. The glasses looked brand new. Dad, this wasn't the first time we've noticed her stealing something. I'm pretty sure she stole one of my favorite rings, the one from Mimi. And one other time, after we had been at the Dollar General and gotten home, I saw her pull a shirt or jersey out of her waistband."

"If she had stolen that, why didn't the alarm sound when she went through the doors?"

"I'm not sure. The only thing me and Coco thought was she took the tags off before going through the security system."

"Yeah, that's possible, I guess."

They got to the playground and thoroughly looked around but didn't see any signs of her there. They went to the Dollar General, not thinking that she would have gone there, but still checked. The clerk was different than the other day, but she said she hadn't seen any young girls that fit Lexi's description come into the store within the last few hours. Ralph gave the clerk his cell number.

"If you do see someone that might favor her, would you mind calling me at this number?"

"Is she in some kind of trouble or something?"

"Oh no. We just haven't heard from her in a couple of hours and were trying to help her Mom find her. She probably just lost track of time."

The store employee said she'd call if she saw her. They told her thanks.

They took a look in the downtown area but didn't see her there either.

"I don't know where else to go, Court, unless you can think of somewhere. I guess we'll head back home. Call your Mom and ask if they've heard from her."

"Yessir."

Neither had heard anything from Lexi. Candi was panicking and Melinda was doing her best to keep her calm.

"Maybe we should call the police," Candi said.

"We can, Candi, but when we tell them that she's only been missing for three or four hours, they most likely won't do anything."

"I guess you're right, Mel. I'm so worried. Why would she be doing something like this? It's all my fault."

"Candi, come on. Don't be so hard on yourself. Lexi and you have gone through a rough patch over the last couple of years. She'll walk through that door any minute. She just had to let off some steam from the argument."

"I guess I shouldn't have tried to force her to go to church. It's just that I want her to realize, like I've begun to, that she needs to let Jesus be in control of her life," Candi responded.

Melinda said, "Lexi might have to see the genuine change in your life before she moves toward Jesus. That might take some time. Every individual comes to Christ differently."

"Yeah. You're right. I just see her headed down a road that will cause her a lot of grief and hurt. I don't want her to have to go through that."

"I know, sis, but some people have to go down before looking up. I agree that we don't want Lexi to be that person, but we can only pray and leave it in God's hands."

Ralph and Courtney walked through the door. Ralph saw a slight glimmer of hope on their faces and was sad to give them the unpleasant news.

"Sorry, no sign of her."

"Do you think we should make the police aware of Lexi being gone?" Melinda asked.

Ralph responded, "Well, the police usually don't do anything until someone has been missing for at least twenty-four hours."

Candi was just sitting on the couch, sniffling with her face in her hands. "I can't just sit here. So I will drive around and see if I see her anywhere."

Ralph and Melinda offered to go with her. She was grateful but objected.

"You two have to get some sleep so you can go to work tomorrow. It'll be good to be out there looking and doing something."

"Okay," Melinda responded, "But be careful. If you find out anything, please call us. We'll be praying."

"Thanks, sis."

Candi got her purse and keys and drove out into the night, hoping to find her daughter. Ralph, Melinda, and Courtney prayed that the Lord would resolve this terrible situation.

As Candi was driving, she began talking to the Lord.

"Father, and I call You that because I know I'm one of Your children. I remember asking You into my life many years ago. Thank You for saving me back then. I'm so sorry for how I turned away from You and followed my ways rather than Yours. I knew better, Lord, but I allowed my own selfish desires to get in the way of You leading me. Again, I'm so sorry and thank You so much for Your forgiveness to this prodigal child. Thank You for leading me back to You. I pray that I will continue to follow Your ways. Get me back into the Word, regularly communicating with You and into a good fellowship of others who want to serve You. Father, I bring my little girl to You this morning. I'm so scared for her. I know You're watching over her, and I'm so thankful I can trust in that. Keep her safe from any harm and from anyone influencing her in the wrong direction. Please, help us to find her. Thank You, Jesus. I love You so much."

Chapter Eight: Runaway

Lexi looked at her cell and saw she had been gone for over two hours. Since she left, she had been in a convenience store where she stole some crackers and a drink and then went to the playground and hung out there awhile. She was there when Courtney and her dad were looking for her, but she had hidden Courtney's bike where it couldn't be seen and stayed out of sight behind one of the trash dumpsters until they left.

She rode by the Dollar General, and it had to be pure luck, she thought, because she saw Ralph and Courtney driving away as she pulled around from the back of the store. She then saw the same clerk she had an altercation with earlier walking out of the store. Lexi, again, stayed hidden until the clerk drove away.

Lexi guessed she must have just gotten off from her shift, which gave Lexi a perfect opportunity to do some hand-grabbing inside the store. She stepped inside, and the clerk behind the counter said hi. Lexi politely replied to make a good impression and not raise suspicion.

She even asked the clerk if they had any chocolate cherry ice cream as if that was what she was looking for. The clerk wasn't sure but told her where to look. Lexi strolled over to the frozen lockers and then moved throughout the store. She ensured that everything she was stockpiling had the alarm bar code taken off or scratched off so the alarm wouldn't go off when she walked through the entrance.

She packed in her pockets and her pants as many items as possible. It was Christmas time for her, and she loved every minute. She stashed underwear and socks, a couple of activewear shorts and shirts, and was even able to pack away a couple of cans of beer and snacks. She wished she could have gotten a couple of packs of cigarettes and a lighter, but they were behind the front counter.

When she got to the counter, she had a cola in her hand, as if she was going to purchase it.

"Oh, I forgot my wallet. I'll be right back."

She, of course, was lying, but the store employee didn't think anything about it. Customers forget their purses and wallets occasionally. The clerk looked at Lexi and wanted to ask if she was the girl Ralph and Coco were looking for, but she thought she'd ask her when she came back in. So, Lexi headed for the entrance, and apparently, she hadn't gotten all the alarm bar codes off of all the items she stole because the alarm rang out loud and strong as she went through the security system.

The store employee and Lexi looked at each other for a split second, and Lexi took off running. The clerk yelled at her to come back, but by the time the clerk got around the counter and out the door, all she could see was Lexi running away. Lexi would have to come back for Courtney's bike later that night. The clerk immediately called her supervisor about the incident.

"Was it a girl about 5' 8" or 9," auburn hair and sleek build?"

"Yeah, that sounds about right." She was surprised that her supervisor nailed the girl's appearance.

The supervisor told the employee, "She was in the store earlier today and stole something." The supervisor continued and let a few expletives fly, revealing her frustration with Lexi.

"Well, there's nothing you can do now." The supervisor ended the call and cursed under her breath again.

Unfortunately, the store employee forgot to call Ralph. After running for ten minutes, Lexi found a house for sale in a neighborhood cul-de-sac nearby. Making sure no one saw her, she went around the back, opened the backyard gate to the wooden privacy fence, and sat on the patio. The Dollar General would close in thirty more minutes; then, she would return and get Courtney's bike. She laid out all her stolen goods and was surprised that she hadn't lost any of the items when she ran away.

She took the jersey and pulled it over her shirt because it was getting a little chilly. After drinking a beer and eating a cold sandwich that she had pocketed, she checked the back door and windows of the house to see if any of them were possibly open. They weren't. She could fix that, however. She broke one of the windowpanes, unlocked the latch, pulled up the window, and crawled inside. She used the bathroom toilet and laid on the carpeted living room floor.

The stolen shorts, underwear, shirts, and socks worked for a pillow. She dozed off a couple of times, but dogs barking and various vehicles driving up and down the neighborhood road woke her up. Finally, after a short rest and letting her food settle, she crawled out the window and returned to Dollar General.

To stay as unnoticed as possible, Lexi stayed off the main road walking behind the houses in the cul-de-sac. She had to duck behind different storage buildings or trash cans at various times. When dogs barked, lights came on, with those in the houses looking out to see what might be causing the disturbance. She finally arrived at the Dollar General and found Courtney's bike behind the structure where she left it. Before she rode off, she thought, "What do I do now?" One thing was sure: she wasn't returning to the Sims. She had decided that she didn't need anyone but herself. The devil was doing a grand job keeping her self-deceived about her situation. So, she took off toward the city to find somewhere to rest.

Candi pulled into Ralph and Melinda's driveway at about 6:30 am that Thursday morning, when Courtney's parents were waking up. She knocked on the front door. After a moment, Melinda opened it, and Candi immediately apologized for waking her up.

"No, I was just getting up and about to put some coffee on. Would you like some?"

"That would be great. Thanks."

"Nothing, huh?" Melinda asked Candi.

"No. I drove around for a few hours hoping to find her but spent most of my time praying. She's not answering or maybe just ignoring my calls and texts. Of course, her phone might need charging. I've made a mess of things, Mel."

"You have got to quit beating yourself up, sis. Lexi has to take some of the responsibility, as well."

"Yeah, you're right, but if I'd not gotten so far away from the Lord, maybe she would have handled all that has happened better."

"Possibly, but you never know. It's like we discussed the other night. Sometimes a person has to hit rock bottom before looking up to the Lord."

Ralph walked into the kitchen and asked Candi, "Any sight of her?"

"No. I can't imagine where she would be. She's never left for this long without telling me. I don't know what she's thinking."

"So sorry, Candi. Wish there were more we could do," Ralph said while hugging her.

Melinda offered to whip up some breakfast. Candi thanked her but told her that she wasn't hungry.

"I think I'll go get some rest. I hope she'll show up soon. It's not safe to be out in this crazy world by yourself."

Melinda answered her. "Okay, get some rest. We're going to get ready for work. If you hear anything, please let us know."

"I will," Candi replied.

Ralph and Melinda went to work shortly after seeing Candi. Melinda left Courtney a note apologizing for not fixing breakfast and continuing to pray for Lexi and Aunt Candi.

Vicki, Coco's mom woke her up at 8:00 and reminded her that they would clean and straighten the storage room in the garage today.

"I tell you what, Mom. How about you do that while I stay in bed for another hour? If you haven't finished by then, I'll help," Coco said jokingly while pulling the covers over her head.

"I'll tell you what, little Ms. Courtney Anne Lawrence. I'll make a deal with you. I'll clean the storage room myself, and you don't get to play with Courtney Sims for the next four weeks. Deal?"

Coco jumped out of bed and replied. "Mom, you drive a hard bargain."

They both chuckled at their silly conversation.

"Would you like me to scramble up some eggs and toast?"

"No, ma'am. I think I want some cereal."

As Coco was sitting at their bar eating one of her favorite cereals, Lucky Charms, and reading her Bible, she received a call from her best friend. Coco answered.

"Hey, you!" Courtney spoke.

"Hey, you, too." Coco replied. "

"Wait till I tell you what's happened since I talked to you at church. It seems Lexi ran away last night."

"What?" Coco said with amazement.

"Yep. Remember I told you she and Aunt Candi had a huge argument about attending church?"

"Yeah."

"When we returned home from church, Aunt Candi told us Lexi hadn't returned since she left."

"You are kidding? Where do you think Lexi went?"

"I don't know, but my dad and I went out last night to look for her but didn't see her anywhere."

"Have y'all called the police?" Coco responded.

"Dad said that the police don't normally do anything for someone considered missing until that person has been missed for at least twenty-four hours. Mom said that she thinks Aunt Candi will probably go ahead and call this morning anyway to see what they say. Lexi is a pain in the neck, but I hope she's okay. I'd hate for something to happen to her."

"Me, too. Why don't we ride around today and look for her?" Coco asked.

"Sounds like a plan," Courtney answered.

Coco asked, "Why don't you ride over here to my house?"

"Okay. I'll be right over," Courtney replied.

"My plan is working perfectly," Coco chuckled to herself. Courtney would be there in time to help her clean the storage room. "Bahaha!"

Courtney got there a few minutes later to Coco's home. She saw Coco's mom cleaning and straightening the storage room.

"Oh, I get it now," Courtney said. "You wanted me over here to guilt me into helping you with your work."

"What? I would never do such a thing," Coco responded.

"Yeah, right." Courtney snorted. "Ms. Lawrence, why don't you go inside, and we'll take care of this in no time."

"Well, that is so sweet of you, Courtney. But, first, why don't you come inside, and I'll fix you a big breakfast while Coco continues to work?"

"Mom! Seriously?" They all chuckled.

"Thanks for the breakfast thing, Ms. Lawrence, but I had some cereal earlier."

"Mom?" Coco asked, "Courtney and I thought we'd ride our bikes around and look for Lexi. Would that be, okay?"

Vicki responded, "I think that would be alright as long as you don't go somewhere that could be unsafe or risky."

"Aw. Mom, you take all the fun out of everything. We were going to try and find a dangerous gang and interrogate each one of them."

Courtney got into the act and added. "Yeah, Ms. Lawrence. We even thought about going to the trainyard and asking the vagrants that live there if they've seen her."

"Okay, you two."

"Courtney, I expected this kind of sass from our daughter, but you are always so sweet and perfect," Vicki jokingly said.

"Perfect?" Coco almost choked on the swig of water she just swallowed.

"Your mom knows me well, Coco."

They all laughed at their silliness.

The girls finished the storage room task in forty-five minutes, and Vicki was impressed.

"Girls! What a great job. Thank you so much for getting this done. It has been an eyesore. How about I give you a twenty-dollar bill so you can get something to eat later while you're out looking for Lexi? I'll be praying that you find her."

Both girls were elated and told Vicki thanks. Then, they got on their bikes and rode away, hoping to find Lexi or at least a trace of her that would help them see where she might be.

Lexi was awakened by the garbage truck lifting the nearby dumpster to empty its smelly contents. She had slept in the back of the building of a small café. She would have gotten quite cold except that she had found a few cardboard boxes. She broke them down and laid some under her and some on her. Not only did it help keep her somewhat warm, but it kept her unnoticed. Every now and then she had to brush off a roach, which really grossed her out. She looked at her cell and saw that it was 9:15 am, and she only had one battery cell left. She was going to have to find somewhere to get it charged up.

She entered the café's restroom to freshen up and use its toilet. Lexi felt okay other than slightly tired and a little sore from sleeping on the ground. She was getting hungry. The last thing she had eaten was the crackers she had stolen. It was time to determine her options. She only had two. She could return to her mom and the Sim's home. Two, she could continue living out here and doing her own thing. She missed her mom but didn't want to go back to live with her because she was doing that religious junk now, and she didn't want any of that. That life was bogus and not for her. So now she's got to find ways to earn money and have that to survive. She pulled Courtney's bike from under the cardboard boxes, got on it, and started riding.

Coco and Courtney rode to Dollar General first. They went inside and asked the clerk who had encountered them if she had seen her.

"No, but my employee from last night did. She stole more items and ran out of the store. Is she a friend of yours?"

Courtney answered. "She's my cousin from Tupelo. She and her mom have been living with my family this week because their house burned down. We're out looking for her because she ran away last night."

"Well, I'm sorry to hear about them losing their house, but it doesn't give her the right to be stealing."

"Yes, ma'am. You are exactly right, and we are very sorry about that."

Coco interjected. "Do you know what she stole? We would like to get money to pay the store back."

"That's mighty sweet of you two, but we'll be okay. You all just find that girl and get her straightened out before she lands herself in jail. She seems to be on the road to destruction."

The girls agreed with the store clerk and told her thank you. Then, outside the front of the store, Courtney asked Coco. "Where do we go from here?"

"I don't know. Let's think for a moment. If we had run away, where would we go?"

Courtney thought for a time and then answered. "Well, a lot would depend on if we had money. But unfortunately, I don't think she has much, if any."

"Okay. So, she's probably getting hungry unless she stole enough snacks to get her by for now."

"Yeah. Let's see." Courtney thought out loud while rubbing her forehead. "We could go to the playground and ask if anyone has seen her."

They both jumped on their bikes and headed that way. Only a few people were there, and the girls interviewed each individual, but no one had seen her.

Lexi decided to try a trick she had used at another restaurant in Tupelo a year ago with some of her friends. So, she sat at a table for breakfast at the Main Street Cafe. The server came to her table and asked what she would like.

"Hey, hon. My name is Myrtle, and I'll be your server. What can I get you this morning?"

"Give me that 'Goal Line' special that I saw advertised on the front door."

"Okay. Which meat would you like, sausage, ham, or bacon?"

"Bacon. And give me some chocolate milk."

"Coming right up." As Myrtle walked away, she thought this girl needed to learn some manners. Lexi asked the server as she was turning around. "Y'all got a phone charger in here?"

"Hon, I've got one in my purse. Why don't you give me your phone, and I'll gladly charge it while you're waiting for your order to come up."

"Yeah. That'd be great."

The waitress took Lexi's phone and connected it to the charger she had in the back office of the kitchen. The waitress brought Lexi's food to her table within fifteen minutes.

"What about my phone?"

"Oh, I completely forgot about it. Let me go get it."

Myrtle went to get it, and as she was unplugging the charger, she accidentally noticed one of the texts her mom had sent. It read, "Please, Lexi. Come home. I love you. Mom." The waitress didn't know quite what to make of the text, but it seemed this girl and her mom had had a falling out. She wondered if she should say anything.

Instead, she returned to the table with Lexi's phone and decided not to be nosy.

"Can I get you anything else?" She asked.

Lexi answered with her mouth full of hash browns, "Nope."

Lexi downed most of her food but strategically left just enough for her diabolical plan. Now was the perfect time to return to the restroom and grab that disgusting little object she saw when freshening up earlier. A dead cockroach! It was going to be ideal for her purposes. She left her table and walked into the restroom, and it was still lying on the floor next to the garbage can. She grabbed some tissue paper, picked up the roach, and hid it in the wadded paper. She walked back to her table and stealthily placed the roach under a piece of the bacon that was left. Now she would pull off the best academy award performance anyone had ever seen before.

"Gross! A roach! I can't believe I found a roach in my food," Lexi yelled out.

Myrtle came running over to her table and asked about the problem.

"You don't see it?" Lexi was pointing at the dead cockroach. "Right there under the rest of my bacon."

And then Lexi let out a vast gagging sound as if she were about to throw up.

"Oh, my goodness!" The server exclaimed. "I am so sorry."

"Well, you should be," Lexi countered. "I think I'm going to get sick."

The manager heard the commotion and walked to Lexi's table. After inquiring about the uproar, he profusely apologized and told her she would not have to pay for her meal.

"I would hope not. I should probably receive some type of compensation. This is sickening," Lexi said, still performing like a veteran Hollywood actress.

The manager, attempting to resolve the issue quickly and not to draw any more attention from the other customers in the café, spoke.

"I'll gladly compensate you another meal or the next time you dine with us. We'll gladly do whatever we can for you, ma'am."

Lexi let out a sigh of hesitation and finally agreed that he could give her a gift certificate to use at another time. However, she told him it would be a while before she used it. First, she would have to have time to forget this unfortunate incident. After receiving the certificate, she briskly stormed out and didn't turn back around. The whole time she had a sly grin on her face. She pulled it off like a pro.

The Courtneys had been riding for about an hour. They had no idea where Lexi would have gone, so they decided to go downtown and inquire at as many shops as they thought she might have gone into.

"I hope she's not going into shops and stealing things, but that has seemed to be her action since we've been with her," Courtney said.

"Yeah, I hope not, too. Let's check in this hardware store. If she's camping out somewhere, this is where she could grab some stuff that she could use."

The girls went inside and looked around, and one of the employees asked if he could help them with anything. Coco described Lexi to the young man and asked him if he had seen anyone looking like her. He said no, at least not this morning. They both said thanks and went a couple of stores into the Dress Barn. They went straight to the back counter and asked one of the salesclerks if they had seen anyone that favored Lexi. They struck out again. Again, they said thanks and left.

"What is that smell?" Coco asked.

"That has to be the café across the street," Courtney answered. "It's 12:30. You want to go there and split something?"

"Sounds great to me. I've never eaten there," Coco responded.

"Me either," Courtney replied.

They crossed the street and walked into the front door of the café, and inside, it smelled even more heavenly. Shortly after sitting down, an older woman introduced herself.

"Hi, ladies, I'm Myrtle, and I'll be your server. What can I get you?"

Courtney told her that they probably would be splitting something, which was an item on the menu she suggested.

"Hmm, what about our deluxe cheeseburger? It comes with fries and a milkshake."

"Ooh, that sounds great," Coco said.

Courtney agreed and asked them what type of shake they wanted before Myrtle went to place their order. They both said chocolate. When she returned with the milkshake, she had halved it into two glasses.

"Wow! This is just one milkshake?" Coco asked.

"Well, I fudged a little and made enough for two. Enjoy!"

They both told her thanks. The waitress returned fifteen minutes later with one of the juiciest, scrumptious burgers the girls had ever seen. Myrtle had split it into two plates.

"Yum!" said Courtney.

"I ditto that," Coco agreed with a huge smile.

"I threw a couple of extra fries on there for you, too," said Myrtle. "You all enjoy. I'll check on you later to see if you need anything."

"Thanks," They both responded.

Courtney and Coco finished every bit of their burger and fries and were almost finished with their shakes when the server returned to their table.

"Well, what do you think?"

The girls told Myrtle it was the best burger they'd ever eaten.

"That's what we like to hear. Myrtle said with a big grin. So, are you two just out wasting time today?"

"Well," Courtney started, "We're out looking for my cousin. She and her mom lost their home in a fire up in Tupelo and have been staying with us since last Saturday. You haven't happened to have seen a young teenage girl today, have you?"

"Kinda slim, tall, auburn colored hair?"

Both girls sat up and said in unison, "Yes, ma'am."

Myrtle slid up a little close to the girls and said softly. "If she's the one, she was here earlier for breakfast. She had ordered our 'Goal Line' breakfast special and just about finished eating it all when, unfortunately, she found a cockroach under her last piece of bacon."

"Gross!" both girls whispered.

"Yeah, I agree, but I'm not sure it happened that way. I don't mean to accuse your cousin, but I placed all the food on her plate. I would have seen a roach if you understand what I'm saying?"

"Ms. Myrtle," Courtney began, "We know exactly what you mean. She is quite a character, and she has some very troubling issues. We wouldn't be surprised if she had placed the roach on her plate to get out of paying for her meal."

Myrtle commented back, "That's actually what I and the manager think happened. She made a huge deal about it, and the manager even gave her a gift certificate for the next time she came in to dine with us." "Yep, that sounds just like her," Coco commented.

"I'm so sorry, Ms. Myrtle. She ran away last night, so we're out looking for her."

"You know, I thought something was awry. She asked me if we had a phone charger, and I told her I could hook her phone up in the back with my charger. When I brought it back to her, I accidentally read a text from her mom telling her to come back home. I almost said something to her but didn't want to sound nosy."

"We understand, Ms. Myrtle," Coco said. "We're just so sorry that you had to deal with her."

"Oh, trust me. I've been in this business so long that nothing surprises me."

"When did she leave?" Courtney asked.

"About 11:00 am."

"Thanks so much, Ms. Myrtle. Can we get our check? We need to get back to looking for Lexi. By the way, we'll drop by later to pay for Lexi's meal. How much was it?"

"Oh, don't worry about it. We'll take care of it. Thank you anyway, girls. Let me go get ya'll checked out." The girls paid for their bill and tipped Myrtle $5.00 and got back on their bikes. They stopped at a couple of other stores but received the same response they had gotten earlier—no one, other than Myrtle, had seen her.

They were about to cross the street at the corner when Coco's cell rang. It was her mom. She put it in speaker mode.

"Yes, ma'am?"

"Have y'all gotten any good news?"

"No, ma'am. No one has seen her except for a waitress at the City Café. We just got through splitting a burger, and she told us that someone with Lexi's description had eaten there earlier."

"Well, at least we know she's okay," Vicki responded.

"We sure hope she is. We wish she'd come back. We're scared for her."

"I know you are. We all are. I'll call Courtney's mom and tell her what you all have told me. You two probably need to come back home. It's getting late. You want me to ask Courtney's mom if she can spend the night with us tonight?"

Courtney could hear Vicki's voice on the cell and nodded her head to Coco.

"Yes, ma'am. That would be awesome."

"Okay. I'll fix one of your favorite meals tonight. Spaghetti."

"Thanks, Mom. I can't wait. We'll head home. Love you. Oh, wait, mom. Just curious. Did Aunt Candi ever call the police?"

"Yes, so they are aware that she's missing."

"Hopefully, they will find her soon. Love you, and we'll see you soon," Coco replied.

If the girls had just turned around, they would have spotted Lexi not ten feet behind them, hiding behind a sign advertising Clark's Furniture Store. She just happened to be at the same corner where they were. Lexi caught most of the conversation between Coco and her mom since it was in speaker mode. Spaghetti sounded good, and honestly, she envied both Courtney's families. It made her feel good that they were looking for her, but she still wasn't ready to return, if she ever would. Now she had to be on the lookout for the police. That just made her life a little more difficult.

Chapter Nine: Lexi's Money-Making Schemes And The Police

The girls got to Coco's home shortly after talking to Vicki. When they walked into the house, the aroma of spaghetti was simply amazing. Dinner wouldn't be ready, though, for another forty-five minutes when Tim would be home from work. The girls went outside to shoot some basketball.

"Coco, I really don't like Lexi, but I truly am worried for her. You were right the other day when you told her she's headed for some serious trouble."

"I know. I just wish there were something more we could do, Court."

They played a couple of games of 'Horse' and '21' and then decided to go inside to see if they could help Coco's mom. Her mom appreciated the offer and told them she had it under control.

"Well, wait a minute. Maybe I could get two to help with something else. If you two want, you can bake the Pillsbury chocolate chip cookies for dessert. They're in the fridge."

They, of course, jumped on that idea. Coco pulled out a cookie sheet while Courtney turned the oven to 350 degrees. This wasn't their first rodeo. Coco sprayed the sheet pan with some non-stick cooking spray, and Courtney brought out the prized possession of delight and then sang.

"Ahh. Gifts from the cookie gods."

Vicki commented. "You girls are crazy!"

"Yes, ma'am, crazy for these cookies," Coco replied with a huge smile.

They started breaking each individual piece and laying them on the cookie sheet. Every now and then, they would break it off a little and eat it raw.

"Yum!" Courtney said with her eyes closed, expressing great satisfaction.

"I know, right?" Coco replied.

At that moment, Tim, Coco's dad, walked through the front door.

"Smells like Heaven in here."

Coco wasn't the only one who loved spaghetti as one of their favorite meals.

"I'm so glad it's going to be just you and me together tonight, sweetheart."

"Dad, you knew we were here," Coco ran and gave him a hug.

"Hey, Sug. And how are you, Courtney?"

"Doing good, Mr. T."

"Well, pity da' fool who would say otherwise!"

"Honey, you really need to work on your Mr. T impression. It's weak."

"And that was from my wife, with the Hollywood Critic network. We'll be right back after this commercial break. Don't go anywhere. Tim will be doing many more of his fantastic impressions."

They all chuckled at their silliness. Each grabbed a seat at the table and enjoyed the spaghetti till they were about to pop. After the spaghetti, they all helped clean everything up. Then Vicki poured everyone a glass of milk and brought the plate of chocolate cookies as they sat together and watched 'Night at the Museum,' which the girls had only viewed about a million times. About 10:30 they all went to bed. It had been a long, exhausting day and both girls fell right to sleep after they had their prayer time.

Early Friday morning, Candi went to the police station and talked to them about Lexi being gone since Wednesday evening. One of the sergeants took her information, got a recent picture of Lexi, and put out an all-points bulletin.

Hopefully, they would find her, and things could get back to normal real soon when she got back to the Sim's home. She decided to do some things to show her appreciation for all the kindness they'd shown her and Lexi this week. She did a deep clean at the Sim's house, cleaned the inside and outside of all their windows, and straightened up the items in their garage. Melinda pulled into their driveway just about the time Candi was finishing up the garage.

"Girl, what are you doing?"

"Oh, I thought I'd do some things to help you and Ralph. You two have been incredible to me and Lexi this week. It's the least I could do to show my appreciation. It also helped take some of my concerns off of Lexi."

"Completely unnecessary, sis. You shouldn't have worked this hard."

As Melinda walked through the back door, she smelled something delectable in the kitchen. "What is that smell?" Melinda asked Candi.

"I just whipped up some chicken dish I used to make. It's really delicious. I think you'll love it." Melinda also immediately could see the evidence of the massive cleaning job that her sister had done throughout the house, as well.

"Candi! You are amazing! I don't think I've ever seen this house look so clean. And the windows, wow!"

"Thanks, Mel. As I said, the least I could do."

"Hey, did you contact the police about Lexi?"

"Yeah."

"What did they say?"

"What I expected. They got a picture of her and supposedly put out an APB, but I'm not sure they take something like this too seriously. Runaways don't seem to be the top priority."

Candi's eyes began welling up with tears and Melinda embraced her and tried consoling her the best she could.

Money! That was the most prominent item on Lexi's mind. She had none and had to get some. She had an idea, but it would be risky. She rode the bicycle to the Winn Dixie grocery store. She walked inside and grabbed a buggy to appear that she was shopping. As she walked down each aisle, she would place an item or two into the shopping cart. At the same time, she was looking for her intended victim, someone with a purse sitting wide open in their cart. She'd never tried this stunt before, but she felt she could do it without any problem. One of the teenagers she was hanging out with in Tupelo told her about the idea. The most important thing was to make sure no one saw her doing it. She found her first victim. Lexi carefully pushed her buggy down the soups and condiments aisle and slithered next to an older woman's cart. There was no one else on the aisle, which made it an even more perfect opportunity. Lexi passed the cart and peered into the lady's purse, which was sitting on her shopping buggy just like a bird perched on a limb, and there was the woman's wallet inside her purse. Lexi had to find a way to distract the older woman so she could grab it.

"Excuse me, ma'am. My mother usually does the shopping for me and my two younger brothers, but she is in bed with the flu, and she asked me to buy some necessary groceries. Would you happen to know where I could find the split pea soup?" The older lady took the bait. "Here, darling. Follow me."

As Lexi followed her, she made sure the lady wasn't looking and reached into her purse and snatched the wallet.

"Here it is, hon. I'm sorry about your mom. I hope she gets well soon."

"Thank you very much. Have a great day."

The older lady walked back to her cart, none the smarter.

Lexi had made a score. She went down another empty aisle, stood close to some canned beans, and looked into her wallet. She grabbed the money, put it into her pocket, and then tucked the wallet into the very back of the shelf behind the Bush's baked beans.

"This was way too easy. There has got to be a couple of more wallets that I can grab before leaving," She thought to herself.

She continued her devious plan walking down each corridor, adding an item here and there into her cart, looking to take advantage of another target. The cookies and snack aisle had one man without a cart and another lady with a shopping buggy. The man seemed oblivious to everything around him, and Lexi wasn't worried about him. The woman wasn't as old as the first one she scored on, but she thought she could still get lucky. Lexi's motive operandi were the same. She passed the lady's cart, and this lady, too, had her purse on the top shelf of the cart, wide open. Lexi used the exact same line with her as she did with the earlier lady, of course asking for finger cookies this time. This lady was much more careful. She grabbed her purse and then showed Lexi where the item was. Lexi told her thank you but was irritated that she wasn't able to get to her purse. Lexi wasn't going to give up yet. As she was going down the drinks aisle, she found another possible prey. This one might be a little more difficult, however. This lady had an open purse, but it was hanging on her arm. As Lexi passed by the lady and peered into her purse, she saw the wallet. Now, how could she distract the woman? She got it. She went to the corner of the aisle where she thought the lady would travel and waited at the end as if she were interested in the endcap items. Sure enough, the lady headed toward Lexi. When she got close to her, Lexi turned quickly and bumped her buggy into hers, making sure it appeared to look like an accident. When Lexi fell into the woman, she reached into her purse at the same time and grabbed the lady's wallet.

"Oh, I'm so sorry, ma'am," Lexi said convincingly. "Are you okay?"

"Yes, and I'm sorry, too. I should have been watching where I was going."

"Oh, I'm sure it was my fault. My mom is sick with the flu, and I don't normally have to do the shopping, but me and my two brothers need some food. I'm not thinking clearly."

Lexi apologized again and pushed her cart toward the other corridors. When the coast was clear, she opened up the wallet, took the money out, and placed the wallet behind some taco seasoning packs.

"Scored again! I better get out of here. I don't want to push my luck," Lexi thought to herself. She left her buggy near the baby items and walked out of the store.

Both ladies ironically arrived at the check-out counters at about the same time. Once their items were rung up, they both reached into their purse and couldn't find their wallet. They could hear each other's conversation with their separate check-out employee and then looked at each other.

The younger one said, "Did a young girl today bump into you accidentally?"

"No, but there was a young lady who asked me if I could help her find a food item?"

"Well, ma'am, I think we were both snookered. I think she distracted us so she could grab our wallets."

"Oh, my, and she seemed like such a sweet girl. She even told me that her mother was sick, and she was doing the shopping for her."

"Yeah. Told me the same thing."

The manager saw the commotion and walked over to the ladies.

"Hi, ladies. My name is Spence, and I'm the manager here. Is there a problem I could help you with?"

Both ladies pulled out of line so the other customers behind them could be served, then proceeded to tell the manager what had happened.

"I am so sorry to hear this. We have security cameras throughout our store, and I will look at the footage and see what I can find. May I have your phone number to call you?"

Both women gave the manager their information and left the store. The manager went to his office to call the police and tell them about the incidents the ladies had encountered. The desk sergeant told the manager that he would send an officer there to look at the video footage with him.

Lexi had ridden down the street and then pulled down a side street where an old-abandoned park was. She got off her bike and sat down on the rusty merry-go-round. She pulled out the money from her pocket to see how much she had gotten.

"Dude!" Lexi said out louder than she meant.

She had ripped off these two ladies for the total sum of $164.00.

"What a day! I can't believe this. $164.00 richer. This is what I'm talking about. It's time to go grab some grub."

Lexi jumped back on the bike and rode to Zaxby's. She loved their chicken fingers and fries. She might even buy a couple of chocolate chip cookies.

Chapter Ten: Police Involvement

Police Officer Hughes met Spence, the Winn Dixie manager in the store office, and they started looking at the video. Spence found the footage where Lexi had met the first woman. They saw Lexi distract the woman so she could reach into her purse and grab her wallet. Another camera view found Lexi on another aisle, taking the wallet out of her back pocket, taking the money out, and then tucking the wallet away behind some of the items on the shelf. They continued observing the footage and discovered Lexi with the two other potential victims she had chosen to swindle. She clearly wasn't successful with one of them because that particular lady took her purse with her when she showed Lexi the item she pretended to need. This, of course, didn't allow Lexi any chance to snatch her wallet. The third intended individual on the video had her purse on her arm, but it was still open. The officer and manager were intrigued by how Lexi waited for her prey at the end of the aisle and maneuvered into position to reach into the lady's purse to grab her wallet. The manager asked the officer.

"What causes a kid like this to do such a thing as rip people off?"

Officer Hughes shook his head and looked at the manager, and said, "It could be various reasons. You never really know why. Sometimes I guess it can be attributed to bad family situations and how they were raised. Peer pressure from their so-called friends can be another reason. Maybe they're in a gang and they have to do something like this as their initiation rite, or perhaps they just have a propensity toward this type of behavior.”

“Sad,” Spence replied.

“I'd like a copy of this video as soon as you can get me one. I will need it if we catch this little thief.”

“I can actually duplicate it right now. It will only take three or four minutes,” The manager responded.

“Great. I'll wait.”

While he waited, Officer Hughes called Candi's cell. He introduced himself and then told her of the incident at the grocery store and that he recognized Lexi as the girl in the video from the picture that Candi had given him earlier that morning.

“Oh no. So, what happens now, officer?” Candi inquired.

“Well, Ms. Patterson, I'll put out an APB, and the different law enforcement groups will be on the lookout for her. If she is found, she'll be taken into custody.”

“Will she have to spend time in jail?”

“I'm not sure about all that. For now, let's just try to find her before she gets into any more trouble. You be sure to call me if you see or hear from her.”

“Yessir, I will, and thank you for calling me.”

"You're welcome, Ms. Patterson." Candi immediately started praying for the police to find her daughter.

The officer took the duplicated video of Lexi's criminal acts and put out another APB, saying that this appeared to be the missing teenager from the earlier APB sent out. The police who were on duty received the bulletin and, during their patrol, kept a lookout for a young teenage girl, about sixteen years old, around 5' 9," with auburn colored hair, wearing light-colored shorts and a navy-blue top.

Chapter Eleven: Lexi's Up And Downs

Lexi hadn't been this happy in a long time, although her happiness was based on unreal expectations. She knew deep down what she had done was wrong, but she didn't care. She felt that life had dealt some really bad hands to her lately, and it was time she got something that felt good. And she was feeling good. She thought to herself.

"Nothin' better than Zaxby's chicken fingers dipped in buffalo sauce. And, boy, do I love their fries. Now to dig into not one, but two chocolate chip cookies. This is perfect."

Unnoticed by Lexi, two teenage boys parked their bikes outside, walked into the restaurant, and went to the counter to give the counter employee their food orders. One of the boys nudged the other.

"Hey, check out the chick in the booth over there. She's looking pretty fine."

The other boy turned around and replied, "Yeah, she'll do."

"She'll do? She's hot," the other boy replied.

"You think every girl is hot," the other teen replied.

"Shut up!" the other teen said, "After we get our food, let's go sit with her."

"Whatever."

They grabbed their trays of food, strolled over to where Lexi was seated, and set their trays down. Lexi had seen all this before, so it didn't surprise her when they made their approach.

"Hey, looks like you could use some company," said the teen who was most interested.

Lexi slowly looked up and responded. "I'm about to leave, and I got plenty of company, and they're not losers like you two."

"Sassy! I like that. What's your name?" one of the boys asked.

Lexi shot up out of the booth and started to leave. She had no intention of talking to these two. As she took her second step, her ankle caught the intentional ankle of that same teen. She fell to the floor, and the boy bent down, acting as if he was going to help her up, but instead, he looked deep into her eyes and spoke.

"I ain't no loser, and if you ever say that again about me or my bestie over here, I will make sure you never call anybody a loser again, capiche?" Lexi jerked away and stood up. She wanted to make a crude remark to both of them but thought better of it. She didn't know if the kid would make good on his threat or not. When she reached the door, however, she yelled out to them, "Losers!" She jumped on her bike and rode away as fast as she could.

The boys left their food on the table, grabbed their bikes, and took off after her. Lexi was fast but not fast enough. They finally caught up with her. They knocked her off the bike, threw her down, and held her to the ground.

"You want to say that again, sweetheart?"

"I ain't your sweetheart, loser," Lexi boldly said.

The boy backhanded her across the face. Lexi felt a sting and a trickle of blood oozing from her lip.

"Hold her arms down, Charlie. I'm gonna see if she has anything worth taking."

He started rummaging through her pockets and found the money, all $164.00 minus what she had spent at Zaxby's.

"Whoa! Lookie here, Charlie. What did you do, girl, rob a bank?"

"Give it back," Lexi yelled.

"Well, now, little girl. I don't think you're in much of a position to be telling us what to do. In fact, Charlie, the way I see it is that we are entitled to this money since she let her smart mouth run all over the place. Wouldn't you agree?"

The other boy didn't say anything. Then the one threatening Lexi said, "Maybe this will teach you a lesson."

Lexi then lowered her tone and tried another tactic. "Please give it back. It's my grandmother's. I just cashed a check for her so she could have some cash. Please."

"Oh, you're good. You really should go to California and become an actress. Your acting skills could use some work, but you might become famous one day. But for now, tell your grannie that we got her money and will be using it for our purposes. Now, you better get your tail outta here before we do something we just might regret."

As much as Lexi wanted to fight, she knew it would be a losing battle. She stood up, brushed off her clothes, and walked away as the boy kept on mocking her.

Melinda, Ralph, and Candi had just finished their supper and sat down in the living room. "Candi, you seem to be holding up pretty well, especially with you finding out about the grocery store incident."

"Even though I didn't think Lexi would go those kinds of extremes, I guess knowing that she is alive and not harmed helps me make it. Of course, it's been amazing the peace that the Lord has given me."

Ralph interjected, "What about we three take a drive around town? Maybe by chance, we'll see her."

Candi responded. "Thanks, Ralph, but we'd probably just waste gas. The police are supposedly looking for her. I just hope they find her before she does something else foolish."

Lexi's pride was seriously injured, but more than that, she couldn't believe that the money she scammed was gone. She thought about how she could be feeling on top of a mountain and then, in one minute, be completely down in the deepest garbage dump. She had to come up with another idea to get money. She thought she could go back to Winn Dixie, but that might be too risky. Someone might recognize her from being in the store earlier. She rode around on Courtney's bike and continued brainstorming.

Lexi didn't like the idea that just came to her, but she was getting desperate and decided to go for it. She didn't know how it would work, but why not try it? She rode over to the Walgreens and stood outside. When customers went in and out of the location, she would tell them that her car ran out of gas down the road and would ask individuals for gas money. After standing outside for a little over an hour, she actually pocketed $67.00 until the manager of the store asked her to leave the area. It wasn't $164.00, but she could think of other ways to make money later. That is when she finds a place to bed for the night.

The Courtneys just finished battling it out on the basketball court. After their third game, they told Coco's parents that they were going to goof off in her bedroom. They got cleaned up, brushed their teeth, put on their pajamas, and jumped into bed. They both were playing some games on their phones when Courtney said with a worried look.

"Coco, I'm scared for Lexi. I called Mom when you were in the shower and asked her if they'd heard from her, and they hadn't."

She told Coco about the incident at the Winn Dixie.

"I can't believe Lexi would do something like that. She really is going to get into some serious trouble," Coco responded.

"Yeah, I know. Why don't we look for her again tomorrow?" Courtney asked.

"Absolutely."

They loved Bible trivia, and they decided to challenge each other before going to sleep. It was a great day spent with each other, and now they were ready for bed. They prayed together for Lexi.

"Night," Coco said, and Courtney answered the same.

Chapter Twelve: New Sleeping Quarters For Lexi

It was close to 7:00, and Lexi didn't like spending the night out in the open, so she started thinking of other ideas where she could go for some sleep. Earlier that evening, Lexi had noticed a 24/7 fitness facility. Of course, she didn't have a membership key, but she had an idea that might work. It was only a few couple of miles from where she was, so she began riding in that direction.

"Oh, crud!" Lexi had just seen the two punks from Zaxby's that harassed her and stole her money earlier that day. She took a quick right into another road, but it was too late. They spotted her, and she knew it. Lexi had to think and had to think quickly. She couldn't let them catch up to her again and take the money she had just conned people into giving her. She looked behind her, and they hadn't made the turn yet, so she took another turn down the next road. She heard them yelling at her.

"Might as well give it up, little girl. You ain't fast enough to run from us."

She saw an older man and woman walking on the sidewalk on the other side of the road. Lexi rode toward them, stopped, and with another academy performance, she pleaded.

"Please help me. There are a couple of boys chasing after me. They grabbed me earlier today and tried to rape me. Thank the Lord, I was able to get away. Please help me, please."

As soon as Lexi had finished pleading for her life, the boys turned the corner. They saw her with the older couple and decided to ride on by. They thought they might have another opportunity to get her.

Once they were out of sight, the lady asked her where her parents were.

"Well, I don't have any parents. I live with my grandmother. Earlier today, I was buying some groceries for her and was going back to her house when those boys chased after me. When they caught me, they started groping and grabbing at me. I was so scared. They knocked the food and stuff out of my arms, and it went everywhere." Lexi thought she would take advantage of this opportunity and try to earn some more money. "They even took the leftover money from my pockets. An older man saw what was going on and told the boys to leave me alone. They let go of me, got on their bikes, and rode away. I thanked the older man, and that's when I ran away. I was so shocked I didn't even think about picking up the groceries that I'd bought for Grandma. I just wanted to get home. I think most of the stuff was ruined anyway. I went back to the grocery store to see if I could get some groceries on credit, but they said they didn't do that. As I was leaving the store, that's when the boys saw me again. Thank goodness you two were here. I don't want to even imagine what they would have done to me. You two have been very kind."

Lexi hoped she hadn't poured it on too thick, and apparently, she hadn't. They offered to give her some money to buy the groceries that she had lost.

"Oh, I could never let you do that," Lexi lied.

"Please. We want to help. In fact, we will even go to the store with you."

Lexi's plan was going awry, but she stayed with her same narrative.

"No, no. Really. Thank you, but you two have already been too kind."

At that moment, the lady's cell phone rang. It was their babysitter calling about some emergency, and they had to go back home. The man looked at Lexi and gave her a one-hundred-dollar bill.

"Here, please take this. We want you to buy you and your grandmother some groceries."

Lexi was able to pull fake tears from somewhere and hugged the man saying over and over, thank you two so much.

"You just be careful, honey," the lady replied to Lexi. "We're sorry that we have to go, but our babysitter said she needed us."

"Thank you again, and may God bless you both," Lexi replied, thinking that was a really nice touch. As the couple walked away toward their vehicle, Lexi thought, "I'm three dollars better than the original amount I had earlier today. Pretty cool!"

Candi crawled into bed and began praying.

"Lord, I'm so scared for my little girl. Please protect her from any harm. Do what You have to do to get her attention. Please, bring her back to me. I love You so much and thank You for hearing my prayer."

She took her Bible out and read until she fell asleep.

Lexi knew she had to be extremely careful not to run into the two teenage boys, but her plans of going to the 24/7 fitness facility were still in play. On her way, she stopped at a convenience store and stole another beer and some cookies. The store employee hardly noticed her. He never looked up one time because he was so engrossed in playing some game on his cell phone. She finally arrived at the strip center where the workout center was located. She watched as several individuals at various times would use their key cards to go in. She noticed that the door would stay open just long enough for anyone that wanted to squeeze through before it shut. She hid her bike around the back, walked to the front, and waited till someone came to work out. It was about fifteen minutes later that a young Hispanic girl about twenty years old walked by Lexi used her key card, and walked in. That was Lexi's opportunity to get in, as well. Her idea worked like a charm. The lady, nor anyone else, even took note of it. They probably could care less, actually. Once inside, Lexi looked around and only saw five people working out. She pretended to do some workouts at a couple of the exercise machines, and as she did, she looked around to see where she might find an out-of-the-way place to sleep. Lexi noticed a charging station where she could charge her phone, which was great because she only had one battery icon left showing.

She saw some workout mats and was determined to use them later as her bed. She saw a door with a sign that read 'storage.' She made sure no one was watching her, and she peeked in. It was full of workout equipment and other items that didn't currently seem to be being used. This large closet would do quite well. She decided to utilize the center's ladies' locker area to take a shower. Inside the locker room, she rummaged through some of the lockers, found a towel, and found a fresh change of clothes. She came out of the locker room and waited till all the other people had left, which was about an hour or so. She grabbed her fully charged phone, took two blue mats into the closet, locked the door, and laid down for the night. Perfect, she thought to herself. She set her phone to alarm her at 6:00 am. Hopefully, not many people would be there at that time. It didn't take long for her to fall asleep. She was exhausted.

Chapter Thirteen: Saturday, An Eventful Day

Saturday morning came way too early. Lexi's cell phone alarm went off and she stretched long and hard. She was considerably sore from all the activity the day before and the workout mats were definitely a replacement for a Tempur-pedic mattress. She peeked out the door and to her amazement, there were a number of people inside the center working out already. How would she get out of the storage room without it looking suspicious? she wondered. She grabbed the mats, rolled them up, and covered her face as she carried them back to where she got them the night before. No one seemed to even notice her. "Great," she thought, "Maybe I can come back here for another night of sleep. Now for some breakfast."

Coco woke up before Courtney and decided to let her sleep a little longer, so she picked up her Bible and read a couple of passages from Galatians 5:22 – 23. *²² But the fruit of the Spirit is love, joy, peace, forbearance, kindness, goodness, faithfulness, ²³ gentleness, and self-control. Against such things there is no law.*

"Lord," Coco prayed, "Help me to live out these characteristics. I know I can only do that in the power of the Holy Spirit. Thank You, Lord. Also, please watch over Lexi. I pray that You would do whatever You have to do to get her back home. Use me and Courtney in any way. You see fit. In Jesus' name, amen."

When Coco got up to get dressed, Courtney woke up.

"How long have you been awake?"

"Oh, I got up around 4:00 this morning. I ran twenty-six miles, did a complete cross-fit workout, and cooked a seven-course breakfast for the family."

Courtney just looked at Coco with a smirk that told her she was full of baloney.

"Just kidding. I just got up a few minutes ago. You woke me up with your snoring."

Courtney reacted, "I told you before. I don't snore."

"Yeah, and angels don't have wings," Coco answered.

"Whatever. Courtney snarled. I'm hungry and something is smelling really good."

Coco said, "Me too. Let's see if mom is making something."

"Cool!" responded Courtney.

When they walked into the kitchen, to their surprise it was Coco's dad doing the cooking. He had cooked bacon, scrambled eggs, and cinnamon toast. "Dad, you're cooking?" Coco asked her dad.

"Why are you surprised? I can cook."

"Yeah, but I can't remember when."

"Okay, you don't get to eat any of this since you're being so sassy. Courtney, you can eat Coco's part and whatever else you want."

"Dad!" Coco responded, knowing her dad was just kidding.

Vicki walked in hearing their conversation.

"What? You're cooking?"

"What is this?" Tim replied. "A conspiracy?"

Vicki sidled up to him, kissed him on the cheek, and told him thank you.

"Alright everyone, dig in."

As they were eating Coco talked to her parents about her and Courtney going to look for Lexi again today.

Coco's dad asked. "Do you two have some new ideas where she might be?"

"No sir, we just thought we'd ride around the town."

Tim and Vicki agreed it would be okay and, of course, be careful.

Lexi went around to the back of the fitness center and found Courtney's bike. She rode to the local Hardee's and ordered hash browns, gravy, biscuits, and bacon. She only had to wait a few minutes for her food. She carried her tray of food to a nearby booth and after scarfing it all down, she rubbed her stomach. "Now that was a great breakfast. Yum!" When she finished, she saw a seemingly happy family of five stroll into the restaurant. They seemed like they hadn't a care in the world. She was jealous. She would never admit it, but she really missed her Mom. She had to get over it, though. There was no way she was going back to her mom again since she was turning into a religious fanatic. She didn't need her Mom and she sure didn't need a God that turned His back on her and her Mom.

She put her head back on the top of the booth and started giving some serious thought about her future. Short-term plans and long terms plans. Short-term, she knew she had to make more money. Both of her most recent ideas had worked pretty well. She thought she would go to the Piggly Wiggly that she passed coming to Hardee's and work the same plan that landed her $164.00 at the Winn-Dixie. That worked perfectly. Long-term plans were a whole other subject. She knew she wouldn't stay here in this town but where would she go? Maybe Tupelo where she came from, but she would run into too many people that knew her there. She would give more thought to this problem later, but for now, she needed to find some more funds.

Lexi had been gone since Wednesday evening and it was already Saturday, Candi thought to herself. She called the police to see if they had any news, but they didn't. They assured her they were still looking and tried their best to console her saying that they felt she would show up soon. She thanked them and then she spent time in prayer before she left the guest room at her sister's home. She walked into the kitchen and found Melinda sitting at the bar with her coffee and reading her Bible.

"Good morning sis," Melinda said.

"Morning. Can I grab a cup?"

"Absolutely."

"I called the police this morning, but they didn't have any new information."

"Sorry, Mel."

"What do I do, sis? I'm at my wit's end. It doesn't make sense that she would do something like this."

Melinda responded, "Candi, we never know what is going on in a person's head, especially a teenager."

"Yeah, I know, but I thought she and I were close enough to talk about anything."

"Whatever you do, Candi, just don't give up. God is always still in control even when we don't see any improvement in a situation. Ironically enough, I was just reading about Mary, the mother of Jesus. Can you imagine how she, as a teenager, must have felt to know that she was pregnant and now she had to tell Joseph, who she was engaged to, about this? Would Joseph really believe her and this crazy story? And then, as I continued reading, Joseph's initial response to Mary was to break up with her. Thank the Lord he got that visit by the angel who reinforced Mary's story. But they both had to trust the Lord even though they couldn't see the end result."

"Mel, I'd never thought of that. That had to be extremely difficult for them."

"No doubt, sis. The Lord knows how difficult this is for you, too. He loves you and is working in this nightmare."

Ralph walked in and grabbed a cup of coffee and asked how Candi was doing and if she'd heard any news. Candi reassured him she was doing the best she could and got him up to speed on the information she had gotten from the police. He asked her if there was anything he could do for her, and she thanked him but there was nothing. They all sat together in the kitchen with their faces full of discouragement and frustration.

Chapter Fourteen: Courtney And Coco The Detectives

Coco and Courtney woke up a little earlier than normal to get started with more of their detective work. The girls rode to Courtney's house to get her dad's bike, which she was very thankful for. Riding that little bicycle was a disaster. They started with that same Dollar General to ask the store manager and employees if they had seen Lexi any other time. They saw the manager and asked her.

"No, and I better not. If I ever see her, I'll make sure the police find her and she'll spend some time in jail, I hope."

They both told the store manager that they were very sorry again for what Lexi had done. They left the store and rode to the main street downtown. They didn't think that she would go into Tony's Pizzeria again, but they did and asked Kevin if he had seen her. Another no, so they left and went into some other stores on the main street and asked store employees if they had seen her.

They passed the 24/7 fitness center and didn't really think Lexi would have gone there but they were not going to leave any stone unturned. Good detectives never did. They knocked on the door and asked if the manager was there. The lady who had stopped working out to open the door explained to them there was no need for a manager. There were just members who worked out there at various times. She told them she hadn't seen anyone like Lexi. The lady turned around and asked Barry, a young man who was the only other one working out in the center at that time, if he had seen any teenage girl lately that wasn't a regular. He got off the treadmill he was using and walked to the front door. Wiping the sweat off his brow he spoke to the girls.

"Hi, girls. I don't know if the girl you're talking about is the one I saw here last night, but I'd never seen her before. She was acting very curiously, but I thought it might have been because it was her first time here. I didn't want to say anything to her because I didn't want her to think I was hitting on her or anything like that. I left probably thirty minutes after she came in."

"Do you remember what time it was when you left?" Coco asked.

"Hmm, if I were to guess, I'd say around 10:00. I hope that helps. I gotta get back to my workout."

"Thanks," both Courtneys responded.

Courtney looked at Coco and asked, "What would Lexi be doing at a fitness center?"

Coco responded, "Well, she is an athlete and probably likes working out."

"Well, yeah, but Coco, she doesn't have a key card to get in much less money to join the center. What would she be doing in there?"

At that moment, another young man carrying his gym bag pulled out his key card and opened the door to the center. The Courtneys both noticed that anyone close enough to the door could have caught it before it closed and walked right in.

"Okay, we know how she got in, but why?" Coco wondered.

They both stood there for a minute and then Courtney said.

"Do you think she went in to find somewhere to sleep?"

"Courtney, you're a genius. That's exactly what she was probably doing. In fact, she could take a shower there, maybe even find some clothes from someone else who works out there and probably grabbed some snacks and drinks they might have available to their members."

"Coco, do you think there's a chance she'll come back here tonight?"

"I know I would. It's pretty safe and you're not outside."

"I need to tell my parents and Candi about this. We need to be here around 10:00 tonight and watch to see if Lexi comes back."

"Great idea, Court. Let's go back to your house and tell your parents and your Aunt Candi." They rode as hard as they'd ever ridden before to Courtney's home. Ralph was out in the yard raking up some leaves and saw them turn into the driveway.

"Whoa, girls. Looks like you're running away from the law."

"Dad, we have a hunch where Lexi might be tonight."

"What?"

The Courtneys were talking at the same time to explain to Ralph what they'd found out.

"Hold on, you two. Let's go inside, sit with Mom and her sister and you two can tell us what you discovered." They hurried inside and immediately started telling them what they had found out.

Candi sat straight up and asked, "So, you say that she might have stayed at the fitness center overnight and might do it again tonight?"

"We don't know, Aunt Candi, but we think it's something we should check on."

"I think you're right. It sure can't hurt, Candi."

"I totally agree, Ralph."

It was only 3:30 so everyone, as anxious as they were, tried to stay busy until later that evening when they would drive to the center. Ralph went back out and raked up more leaves and pine straw, Melinda and Candi replaced some old shower curtains with new ones in both bathrooms that Melinda had wanted up for ages and the Courtneys did some rollerblading and then shot some hoops. After a couple of hours, Ralph came in and suggested they go out to eat. That way they would be close to downtown.

"Maybe there's a restaurant close to the fitness center."

Melinda said, "I think that small cafe called 'Wherever' is close to there. I'll go online and check."

It was always a running joke when someone would ask where they wanted to eat, they would answer, wherever. It was famous to all the locals for its melt-in-your-mouth rolls and homemade salad dressings and their homemade desserts. Melinda looked online and found the address.

"Yep. Here it is. Just a couple of blocks from the 24/7 workout center. I think I'll invite Tim and Vicki to come, as well."

When she asked, they said they would love to and would meet them at the restaurant at 7:45. Everyone got cleaned up and dressed and left for the restaurant around 7:30.

Chapter Fifteen: Lexi And Her Scamming Ways

Lexi had scored again at the Piggly Wiggly. But she had gotten there a little too early. There was hardly anyone there, so she decided to ride around town. She dropped into a Hibbett's Sporting Goods store and looked around. There was only one employee that she could see and thought this would be another chance for her to grab something. The employee was on her cell phone and didn't even notice Lexi. She scavenged around and found a couple of pairs of socks, some shorts, and a cool-looking tee shirt. She was extra careful and made sure the security tags were off the clothing she was going to steal, so the alarm wouldn't go off as she left. Gone without a trace.

Before leaving, Lexi bravely asked the employee if she would give her a bag. She told her that her church youth group was on a scavenger hunt and one of the things she had to get for her team was a Hibbett's shopping bag.

The female teen employee gladly obliged and even said, "Cool."

Of course, Lexi had a whole other purpose for the bag. She went to the public restroom and pulled out the stolen items and placed them into the bag. *Perfect*, she thought. After that, she rode the bike back to the Piggly Wiggly grocery store. It wasn't long before she found an unsuspecting elderly lady who would be her first victim.

As she did at the Winn Dixie the day before, she asked the lady if she knew where a particular item was, and when the elderly lady would leave her shopping cart with her purse open, Lexi would grab the individual's wallet. She was always polite and would thank the people she had duped. Lexi was pushing her luck, but she was able to con three ladies. This time, though, she went into the ladies' restroom in the grocery store and then pulled out all the money out of all three wallets. She really racked up. $215.00! She couldn't believe it.

Uh oh!

As she turned down the aisle from the restrooms, she noticed all three women at the front talking to what looked like a manager. She took off to the back of the store, ran through the door that read 'Employees only,' and looked for a back door so she could go out. Luckily, there was one. She opened it up and the alarm went off, but she didn't care. She ran fast as she could behind some other stores close by. Lexi found a place to lay low behind a dumpster. It stunk to high heaven, and she saw a rat run over her shoes. She screamed and ran toward the drainage ditch behind all the stores. She walked till she was at least a couple of miles from the Piggly Wiggly. The manager of the grocery store called the police station and just like the Winn Dixie ordeal, the video that the manager showed the police officer proved that Lexi was the culprit who had stolen money from the ladies in the store.

Lexi couldn't dare go to the store to pick up Courtney's bike. She could attempt that later. Hopefully, no one will put two and two together to think that it was Lexi's transportation. After an hour or so, Lexi headed toward the fitness center to get cleaned up and some sleep but first, she wanted to try the little café near the workout center. "Wherever!" What a stupid name she thought to herself. Anyway, even though she thought it was a ridiculous name for an eating establishment, she was going to give it a try. She entered the restaurant and a hostess asked her if she had a preference where she'd like to sit.

"How about in the corner over there?"

"Sure," answered the hostess.

Lexi sat down and the server came over and asked her if she'd had time to look over the menu and if she had any questions.

"Nah. Give me the ten-ounce rib-eye with a baked potato. Salad come with that?"

"Yes, ma'am, it does. What dressing would you like?"

"Thousand Island," Lexi replied.

"And what would you like to drink?"

"Coke."

"I'm sorry but we only have Pepsi products."

With a disgusted look, Lexi responded, "Just give me a Mountain Dew then."

"Yes ma'am, and I'll be right back with our famous homemade rolls and some butter."

Lexi looked at her phone and noticed that her mother had called four times and texted three times during the day. Lexi thought about leaving a text just to let her know that she was okay but thought she would let her stew a little longer. She thought maybe it would help her Mom to quit this God thing and start thinking smart. The server brought some hot, steaming rolls and their homemade butter and her salad. By the time Lexi had finished three rolls and her salad, her rib-eye steak and baked potato arrived.

"Is there anything else I can get you, ma'am?" the server politely asked.

With her mouth filled with a huge bite of steak, Lexi just wiggled her head back and forth indicating that she didn't need anything.

As the server was leaving, Lexi yelled out with a mouthful of another roll. "You for some A-1 sauce?" The server didn't understand her and asked again.

"Excuse me?"

"A-1 steak sauce!"

"Yes ma'am. Right away."

Lexi finished her meal in record time. She realized she hadn't eaten all day, so she was awfully hungry. All the walking she had to do since she didn't have Courtney's bike caused her to run off some unnecessary calories. The server strolled back to Lexi's table and asked her if she would like to try one of their homemade desserts.

"Why not? Whatcha got?"

After going through the list of items, Lexi chose the chocolate supreme pie.

"Excellent choice. I think you'll really enjoy it."

Lexi whispered to herself as the server left, "I really don't care what you think," she chuckled at herself.

Lexi heard some people coming into the café and glanced up out of curiosity. She couldn't believe it. Her Mom, Ralph and Melinda, Courtney, and the other brat with her parents. "Great!" she thought. "What do I do now?" Thankfully, the hostess took them to the other side of the room where they had larger tables to accommodate them. She held up the menu that was left on the table and hid her face to see if they would be able to see her. They wouldn't be able to unless they used the restroom, which was close to where she was seated. Maybe she could slip out before that happens. The server brought Lexi her slice of pie and walked away. Lexi ate it and occasionally made a glance toward her Mom to make sure they didn't see her. Truth be told, she looked more often than she meant to just to see her Mom. She really missed being with her. She finished her pie and tried to figure out how to leave without being seen. She thought of a plan but didn't know if it would work or not. It was the only thing she could think of. She knew the longer she stayed in the restaurant the more of a chance her family might see her. The server came to the table with the check for Lexi's meal.

"I go to college at the community college here and my parents who live in Tupelo surprised me and just pulled up outside. Do you mind if I go get them so they can sit with me? My mother is in a wheelchair, and I'd like to help my dad get my Mom in here."

"Sure. That will be fine. I know it'll be nice for them to see you," the server replied.

"Thanks. I'll be right back."

Lexi slipped quietly to the front door without anyone seeing her, at least that's what she thought. Courtney had gotten up to go to the restroom and caught a glimpse of her as she was leaving and she yelled out.

"Lexi."

Her parents, her Aunt, and Coco's parents looked at her and Courtney said, "Lexi just went out the front door."

Ralph and Candi jumped out of their seats and ran out the front door but didn't see her anywhere. They came back inside and asked Courtney if she was sure that it was Lexi.

"Yessir. I know for sure."

The server came over to their table and asked, "Did you know that young girl?"

Candi answered, "Yes, that is my little girl."

"Well, she just stiffed me for $32.00."

Candi walked to her seat and looked in her purse for some money.

Ralph told her, "Don't worry about that Candi. We got it."

Ralph apologized to the server and asked her if she could put Lexi's check on his bill. She said, "Of course," and thanked him.

Lexi was hiding in an entryway of a store a couple of stores down. Once her Mom and Ralph had gone back inside, she decided to walk to the fitness center and get settled in. It was perfect timing because an older fellow was coming out, which allowed Lexi to slip into the center's front door. Luckily, there was no one else working out. Lexi put her phone on the charging table so her phone would be charged when she got through getting cleaned up. She couldn't wait to get into the hot steaming shower. It was so refreshing the night before. She went straight to the ladies' locker room, bathed, and then put on the new clothes she had stolen at Hibbett's earlier. She grabbed the workout mats again, picked up her phone, and went to the large closet she used the night before. After locking the door, she set her alarm for 6:00 am and settled in for the night. She enjoyed watching some TikTok and Instagram videos until she fell asleep. Throughout the night she knew she would wake up like she did the night before because at various times individuals would come in and work out. Nonetheless, she knew she would get a decent night's sleep.

The group thoroughly enjoyed their meal, that is, except for Candi. It was difficult for her to get Lexi out of her mind. To be that close to her and not be able to see her was almost more than she could bear. She had spent a long time in the café restroom crying. Melinda came in to try and comfort her the best she could. After they all had finished their meals, they paid and left the establishment. Tim and Vicki said thanks for inviting them and told Candi that they would continue praying for Lexi and their situation. Candi told them thank you. Courtney went home with them since Candi, Ralph, and Melinda would be doing surveillance on Lexi. Ralph walked back in the restaurant and bought three large coffees. He didn't know how long they would be doing their reconnaissance and they might need it to help stay awake.

Chapter Sixteen: Looking For Lexi

Lexi's Mom, Ralph, and Melinda went to the 24/7 fitness center. It was only 9:30 and if the information that she had entered into the center last night around 10:00 was correct, Lexi could be entering any time now. They stayed in the car for about an hour and there was no sign of Lexi. Candi, being courteous, suggested they leave, but both Melinda and Ralph said they felt they needed to stay a little longer. Another hour passed by as they drank their coffee, and watched various individuals, young and old, go in and out of the fitness center, but never saw Lexi. Candi looked at the time and spoke up again and said they needed to leave. Ralph spoke up with an idea.

"Before we leave, I think I'll knock on the door and see if anyone will let me in. I'll tell the one who lets me in what we're doing, and that I just needed to look around a bit."

"Great idea, hon," Melinda said.

Ralph got out of the car and walked to the front door of the center. A young man opened the door and allowed Ralph in. Ralph spent a few minutes spying out the fitness center's various areas but didn't find any sign of Lexi. He even tried to open the door where Lexi was asleep but, of course, it was locked. Ralph thanked the young man for opening the door and then ambled back to the car with the sad news. They all went home feeling dejected and disappointed. Melinda spoke up, "Maybe we should have thought about this earlier, but do you think a good idea would be to let the police know that we think she might be in the fitness center?"

"I think that would be a great idea."

Candi called and the desk sergeant answered. She told him about the situation, and he said he'd call Officer Hughes, who is handling the case, and tell him your information. She thanked him. The desk sergeant had every indication to call the officer but at that moment another police officer was bringing in a loud, obnoxious drunk to be booked and he completely forgot to call Officer Hughes.

The desk sergeant was leaving his shift at 6:00 am the next morning when Officer Hughes walked through the front door.

"Hey, Hank. The mother of that girl who's missing called last night and told me that she might be staying overnight inside the 24/7 fitness center downtown."

"Why didn't you tell me last night?"

"At that same time, Officer Jackson brought in a loud, disgusting drunk and I had to book the guy for public intoxication and disorderly conduct, and I totally forgot to call you. My bad, Hank."

"I understand, Sergeant. I'm gonna drive over there and see if I can find anything," Hank responded.

Officer Hughes drove to the workout center, which was only a few minutes from the police station. This was the first strong lead he'd gotten to find this irresponsible, reckless teenager. He hoped he had not missed an opportunity to catch her at the fitness center, if, in fact, she was even there.

Lexi's alarm went off and scared her immensely. She was in a very deep sleep and was dreaming that she was being chased by both grocery store managers, the ladies she had stolen money from, and the whole police force. She was on Courtney's smaller bike that she had ridden before. "Whew! That was scary. I gotta get outta here," she thought to herself.

She was frustrated when she looked at her cell phone and saw that it was already 6:20 am. She peeked out the door and the center were loaded with early birds working out on this Sunday morning. She grabbed the mats like she had done the day before and hopefully, no one would notice her. If anyone did, she wasn't aware of it.

She gradually walked toward the front door to not gain any attention and slipped out. At that same time, Officer Hughes stepped out of his service vehicle and was walking to the front door. A young girl was walking up the sidewalk in the opposite direction with her back to him. He wasn't sure it was the girl.

"Ma'am?"

Out of instinct, Lexi turned around. When she saw it was a policeman, she took off running. He recognized her from the videos from both grocery stores and called out for her to stop. She continued and he ran after her. He persisted after her, but she was much faster than he was, so he called for backup on his shoulder mic.

"I'm on foot in pursuit of a run-away teenager who has allegedly stolen money from persons at two of the local grocery stores. She is about to cross Main St. and 3rd."

Lexi hadn't stopped running and she took a quick glance back to see how much distance was between her and the police officer chasing her. She was in the middle of 3rd St. when she turned back around, and a dreadful accident occurred. A driver of a black Ford Expedition saw Lexi but did not have enough time to even slow down. The motorist tragically hit Lexi, threw her up onto the hood of the truck, broke his front windshield, and slammed her violently back on the asphalt.

Curious onlookers who saw the collision gathered around Lexi to see if she was dead or alive. Officer Hughes saw the whole shocking incident. He asked the people surrounding her to move to allow him to see what potential damage and severity of the injuries Lexi might have incurred. He felt for a pulse and at the same time called for an emergency ambulance to come to the scene. He could tell that she had gone into shock and had a shallow rhythm of a heartbeat. Within a few minutes, an ambulance pulled up to the accident scene and did the necessary actions to get her to the hospital quickly as possible.

Candi had left the Sim's home to purchase some coffee and creamer when a few blocks ahead she saw a crowd of people and the emergency lights flashing from a couple of police vehicles and an ambulance. She supposed it was a major accident involving two vehicles and a personal injury. As she arrived closer, she saw the paramedics putting an individual into the ambulance and driving away, apparently to the hospital. One of the other officers who had come to help with the mishap directed her car through and cleared the other stalled vehicles from the area. She received a call on her cell phone at the same time.

"Ms. Patterson?"

"Yes sir," Candi recognized the number was Officer Hughes. She answered with curiosity and hope.

"I'm sorry to inform you of the most recent incident but it concerns your daughter. She was in an accident where she was hit by an individual driving an SUV. She was taken to the county medical center."

"Oh no, no. Is she okay, officer?"

"Ms. Patterson, you'll need to go to the medical center to get that information. They will assess the injuries and will give you the details."

"Thank you, Officer. Could you please give me the address?"

Hank gave her the address and told her he would see her later since there would be criminal issues that he would have to continue investigating, no matter the extent of Lexi's injuries. Candi understood and thanked him again. On the way to the medical center, Candi called her sister, Melinda, and told her the unfortunate news. Melinda told her she would be there as soon as she could. Melinda called Ralph and he said he would meet her there. Melinda thought of calling Tim and Vicki, too, so Courtney would know about the mishap. They were eating breakfast before going to church but decided to meet them at the hospital instead.

Chapter Seventeen: Coma And The Medical Center

Within minutes of each other, Candi was joined at the medical facility by Melinda, Ralph, the Lawrences, and both Courtneys. Since she hadn't heard anything yet from the doctor about the extent of Lexi's injuries, she could only tell them what she knew about the accident itself. They listened intently as she told the different details leading up to the accident and how Lexi was involved in the impact.

Ralph said, "Why don't we gather together and pray?"

They got in a circle and grabbed hands, and Ralph asked Tim to lead in prayer. Tim was glad, and they had a brief time talking to the Lord about Lexi. After praying, they all settled into a chair in the emergency waiting room. After an hour or so a doctor walked into the room.

"Is there a Ms. Patterson here?" Candi quickly got out of her seat.

"Yessir. That's me."

He asked her to step to where he was so he could disclose to her the details of Lexi's medical situation. Candi stepped closer and he began.

"The impact from the vehicle caused some serious complications. Your daughter has two broken ribs on her left side and her left femur was broken as well. In addition to that, her brain started to swell so we had no other option but to give her a medically induced semi-coma. That will keep the swelling down and will hopefully slow any further potential hemorrhaging. It will also help her body to rest and heal at a slower and safer pace."

"When would you take her out of the coma?" Candi inquired.

"That's up to your daughter. What I mean by that is as long as her body responds to the medication, then it shouldn't be too long before we would wake her up. A young body usually doesn't need to be in a comatic state for a very long because their body responds and heals quickly. Let me get back to the team who is with her, and I'll be sure to talk with you later."

"Thank you, doctor."

The family stood up and walked to a sullen and saddened Candi and asked her what she found out from the doctor. With tears streaming down her face and Melinda hugging her, she proceeded to tell them what the doctor said. They all did their best to support her and help her handle the news about Lexi, but it was probably the most challenging experience Candi had ever had to suffer. There was little anyone could do but pray and wait. The doctor came out within the hour and told Candi that Lexi had been stabilized and it would probably be best for her to go home and get some rest, and he would keep her informed on any improvement. With that, she and the others left the medical center to go to their homes.

Ralph asked Candi, "Candi, do you mind if I inform our pastor of everything and ask him to let our congregation know so they can start praying for the situation?"

"That would be wonderful, Ralph. Thank you."

Ralph immediately called their pastor and informed him of the full spectrum of the Lexi situation.

"I'm so sorry to hear all this, Ralph. Is there anything I can do?"

"I don't think so, Preacher, other than getting the word out on our Facebook page and asking our congregation to start praying for Candi and Lexi?"

"Great idea, Ralph. I'll put it out there ASAP."

Sundays were supposed to be a time to attend church, watch some ball games later, and just enjoy relaxing with family and friends, but this Sunday was filled with gloom and sadness. Melinda nor Ralph knew what to say to Candi because of all the unknowns in this recent situation with Lexi's accident. Still up in the air were the legal ramifications and consequences that Lexi would have to face with the crimes she had committed once she recovered from her injuries. It was close to 6:00 pm and Melinda commented.

"I'll make some supper for us. How does taco salad sound?"

Courtney and Ralph answered that that sounded good, but Candi didn't respond, which was expected. Courtney heard her cell ring in her bedroom and left the show she was watching on TV in the den.

"Hey, you!" Coco said.

"Hey, you" Courtney answered.

"Just thought I'd call to see how you were doing."

"Thanks, Coco. I'm okay. Worried for Lexi, of course. I'm also concerned for my Aunt. She's really in a deep funk right now."

"Yeah. I can only imagine. This is gotta be really tough for her."

"Yeah. She's just been sitting on the bed and crying in our guest room."

"So sad. We just have to keep on praying that the Lord would do what He does best."

"Yep. Hey, Mom is calling me. I'll holler at your later. Thanks for checking with me. Love ya, girl"

"Love you, too, Court."

Courtney walked into the kitchen to see what her Mom needed.

"Sweet, will you set the table for supper and then pull out the lettuce and tomato that's in the fridge?"

"Sure. Smells wonderful. I love taco salad."

Melinda smiled at her. After a few more minutes everything was ready.

"Court, go tell your dad that supper is ready. He's in the garage doing something."

"Okie dokie."

Melinda went to the guest room door and knocked on it. Candi answered to come in. Melinda sat next to her on the bed and put her arm around her.

"Come on and eat something."

"I'm not really hungry, sis."

"I know, but you've got to keep up your strength and you haven't eaten anything all day."

"I'm okay. I just prefer to be alone right now."

Melinda thought about pushing harder for her to eat but decided that Candi did need time alone for now anyway. She would check on her later.

"I love you, sis. Call me if you need anything," Melinda said as she left the guest room.

"Whatcha working on, Dad?" Courtney asked.

"Just putting up some more shelves so we can get some of this stuff off the floor."

"It's looking good. Mom wanted me to tell you supper is ready."

"Great. I'm starving."

Ralph, Melinda, and Courtney didn't say much to each other during the meal. They would have enjoyed the taco salad more if the conditions of the evening weren't so grim. They reminded each other to continue praying. After thirty minutes or so they had finished eating. Courtney and Melinda cleared off the table and cleaned the kitchen while Ralph went back out to the garage to finish the project he was working on. Courtney turned on the TV to watch a movie and Melinda sat with her. The atmosphere in the house was filled with hopelessness and despair. Candi hadn't been out of her room since they all had come back from the hospital. Melinda brought a plate of food to the guest room, knocked on the door, and sat it down on the bedside table.

"Sis, here's you a plate. Please eat. It'll make you feel better."

Candi looked up at her sister with bloodshot eyes and burst into tears again.

"What going to happen, Mel? I'm so scared for my little girl."

Melinda sat down beside her and squeezed her tight.

"All we can do now is leave it in the hands of the Lord."

"Why would He allow this to happen? He could have kept her from getting hit by that car. He could have kept her from running away and doing all the wrong things she'd been doing."

"I understand your questions, Candi, but the Lord allows us to make our own decisions. We're not robots. He gives us the opportunity to make good decisions and bad ones. He doesn't force us one way or the other. And as you and I know, our choices determine what happens to us."

Candi didn't seem convinced and through her sobbing, she responded, "I know you're right, sis, but it's just so hard to accept."

"Candi, I totally understand. Remember the miscarriage I had a couple of years before I had Courtney? It was one of the worse times in my life. I thought I'd never get over losing our baby. As much as Ralph tried to console me and tell me that God was in control and that we can't understand why He allows certain things to happen, I didn't want to accept his attempt at comforting me. I'm sure that's how you feel now."

Candi just nodded her head and continued weeping. "It just doesn't seem fair, Mel. Lexi is a good girl. She's just lost her way recently."

"You're right, sis. But sometimes the Lord uses our bad choices and circumstances to get our attention. Hopefully, that is what He is doing with Lexi now."

None of what Melinda was saying seemed to be making any impact. She hugged Candi and said she would leave her alone and to please call her if she needed anything.

Chapter Eighteen: Waiting Is The Worst, But Prayer Is The Best

It had been a long three days. Lexi was still in her coma and hadn't shown any sign of recovery. Candi was beginning to lose hope. She had been staying in the room with her daughter at the medical center since Sunday evening. She was completely exhausted but being close to her daughter gave her a small sense of comfort.

Candi bowed and prayed, "Father, I'm really struggling with this whole situation. I know You're in control, but I'm losing the strength to hang on with believing that. Please help me with my unbelief."

She picked up her Bible and read a couple of chapters, but nothing brought any relief. She was getting more and more discouraged. Ralph and Melinda dropped by the medical center after work and brought Candi some food from Chic-Fil-A. She was very appreciative. Melinda sat down beside her on the couch that was in the room.

"Any noticeable improvement?"

Candi just shook her head no.

"Y'all shouldn't be here. Don't you have church tonight?"

"Ralph answered, "Yeah, but we thought it'd be best to be here with you. Tim and Vicki picked up Courtney so she could go."

"You two have been amazing throughout all this. I'm so sorry that you've had to deal with it," Candi replied.

"Seriously, sis? We love you and Lexi and would do anything to help. I know it's difficult to see any good from all this now, but I can sure say that I'm very glad you two are back in our lives."

"And I concur," Ralph chimed in.

Candi smiled and gave her big sister a long hug.

Tim, Vicki, and both Courtneys arrived at the church a little later than normal. It was probably close to 6:45 and the different services started at 6:30. They noticed that everyone except the children had gathered in the sanctuary. The pastor had cancelled the normal schedule except for the children and had everyone join together to pray for Candi and Lexi. After he shared with the diverse group that was there about the events that had led up to the situation, he asked them to gather into small groups and pray for them. With some soft praise and worship music in the background, the season of prayer was incredible.

After about fifteen minutes the pastor shared a passage found in Philippians 4:6 – 7. *Do not be anxious about anything, but in every situation, by prayer and petition, with thanksgiving, present your requests to God. And the peace of God, which transcends all understanding, will guard your hearts and your minds in Christ Jesus.'*

'Paul wrote this to the Philippian Christians. They were going through difficult times, persecutions from Jews and Gentiles alike, disagreements about doctrine, and other struggles a new group of believers would encounter so this encouragement and exhortation from Paul was necessary. But it wasn't only for them, but for us as well. We all have experienced difficulties that brought about anxiety, lack of peace, stress, depression, and discouragement. And hopefully, we have learned that the most significant option we can choose is go straight to God and trust Him with the situation. When we do that, we'll eventually find the tranquility that He promises and a calmness that is completely mysterious and unfathomable to us and especially to those who don't know the Savior. We can be grateful for a God who cares for us so much and knows our every need. Let me close with this scripture found in Hebrews 4:15 – 17. *For we do not have a high priest who is unable to empathize with our weaknesses, but we have one who has been tempted in every way, just as we are—yet he did not sin. Let us then approach God's throne of grace with confidence, so that we may receive mercy and find grace to help us in our time of need."*

"Thank you all for being here tonight and let's continue to pray for Melinda and Ralph's family. Hope to see you this Sunday morning. You're dismissed."

Tim and Vicki thanked the pastor and told him that Candi will surely appreciate it.

It must have been around 7:00 pm when Candi, her sister, and her brother-in-law saw a movement. They weren't sure but they watched closely to see if what they had seen was correct. There it was again. A twitch of Lexi's right hand. Candi jumped up and grabbed it and started squeezing it hard and saying, "I'm here, baby. I'm here. Wake up. Come on, sweetheart." Melinda and Ralph also drew near Lexi's bed and began praying that she would pull out of her coma. A couple of anxious minutes later Lexi began to slowly open her eyes. Extremely confused about the moment she was experiencing, she thankfully recognized her mom, Melinda, and

Ralph. "Mom?" Lexi was able to express herself in a soft whisper. At that moment, a nurse from the front desk had come into their room because she had noticed Lexi's monitors were creating such havoc. The nurse began her evaluation and saw that Lexi was, in fact, pulling out of her comatose state. She checked all her vitals, and everything looked exceptionally good. The nurse told Candi she would call the doctor and he would be there as soon as possible. Lexi was still groggy and disoriented. Candi did her best to relay to her where she was and to remain calm until the doctor arrived.

The doctor entered their room about thirty minutes later. He, too, evaluated Lexi's vitals and was impressed and grateful that she was doing so well. He told Candi that it would now be a little more of the waiting game to see if she continues to respond to the medication and that he'd be back later that day to check on her. Candi thanked him and continued to hold Lexi's hand and talk to her. Melinda and Ralph decided that it would be a good time to go. They hugged Candi and told her to call them if she needed anything and also what information the doctor would tell her later. She thanked them for being with her and said she would call them later. On the way home, Melinda called Vicki and told her the good news.

"Melinda, that's such good news. How is Candi holding up?"

Melinda replied, "Really good, considering she's obviously excited that Lexi has pulled out of her coma. She seems to be in much better spirits."

"Great," Vicki responded. "I'll tell Tim and Coco. Let us know if we can help with anything."

"Thanks, Vic. Love you."

"Love you, too, Mel."

Ralph thought it would be good to pass the good news to their pastor so he could share it with their church family.

Courtney called Coco once her parents told her the news about Lexi.

"Mom just told me. That is great!"

"Yeah. The doctor said she's not out of the woods, yet, but she's doing better than he expected this early."

"Awesome! God is good!" Coco responded.

"He sure is," Courtney countered.

At the end of the week, Lexi was well enough to go home. It was a beautiful Saturday morning and Lexi and her mom put her items together, got in their car, and drove to her sister's home. Lexi still had some extreme soreness on her left side from the broken ribs and she was learning to maneuver on the crutches for her broken leg. Over the past couple of days, Candi and Lexi had some deep conversations about their personal relationship and made amends with each other. The event that almost had taken Lexi's life seemed to also have an incredible impact on her spiritual outlook on life. She was starting to open up about the Lord and her relationship with Him. Candi was so excited but didn't push the conversation allowing Lexi to talk about it when she wanted to.

They pulled into the Sim's driveway and Melinda, Ralph, and Courtney met them outside and helped Lexi in. It was somewhat awkward at first. Lexi wasn't sure how they would respond to her since she'd left the way she did, and they didn't really know how she would respond to them. You could tell that the Lord was working in Lexi's life. Her whole attitude was different. She seemed humble and broken. The cocky Lexi seemed to be gone and a changed Lexi had entered. She was easy to talk to and her responses were considerate and respectful.

"We're so glad to have you back and so very grateful that you're out of the hospital," Melinda told Lexi.

"Yes, ma'am. I am very grateful, too. I had really gone off the deep end. I don't know what happened. Mom and I have had some good talks and gotten many things out in the open. I'm also going to have to make a lot of what word did you use, Mom?"

"Restitutions."

"Yeah, restitutions with quite a few people starting with you three. Melinda, Ralph, Courtney…I'm so sorry for the way I treated you since Mom and I came here. I was a total jerk. Court, especially to you. You and Coco tried your best to show me friendship, but I just kept on rejecting y'all and your kindness. I'm so sorry."

"Lexi, really, that's okay. I'm just so excited that you're on the mends. In fact, how about a game of basketball? I think I might score a couple of points on you right now."

They both smiled at each other.

"I told Mom earlier this week while we were still at the medical center that I wanted to give my life to the Lord. I'm trying my best to get everything straight. I've got some serious criminal charges that I'm going to have to face which scares me to death, and some people I need to apologize to, but I believe, as Mom has told me, that the Lord will walk us through them. I'm ready to take the blame and pay the penalty for all the stupid choices that I've made over this past week."

"Lexi, I think you are amazing. We all are going to be here for you and help in any way we can to help you through this."

"Thanks, Uncle Ralph."

They all thanked the Lord for His faithfulness and for answering their prayers.

A knock on the Sims' door occurred at that moment. Ralph opened it up and standing there was Officer Hughes. He invited him in and after making his introduction to all in the room he began speaking.

"I'd found out that your daughter was out of the hospital, and I needed to talk with you and her about the issues at hand. Would you like to come to the station and talk or here?"

Lexi had a huge knot slowly rising in her throat. She had no idea what the officer was going to say. Candi looked around and got the assurance from her sister that it would be fine for them to talk there if she wanted.

"Right here will be fine."

"Okay, is there a room that just the three of us can go into?"

Ralph interjected, "Y'all are welcome to stay in here. We'll step outside until you are finished."

"Thanks, Ralph," Candi said.

Ralph, Melinda, and Courtney walked out the back door to the patio furniture and offered up another prayer that the Lord would help Candi and Lexi through this.

"First, let me say that I'm glad you're out of the medical center and I hope you'll continue to heal up quickly from your injuries."

Lexi thanked the officer.

"Lexi, as I'm sure you know, you have some serious criminal charges that have been brought against you by individuals you have stolen from. At this time, I have a manager from a Dollar General store who's made a claim that you shoplifted items from their store and there are four ladies who've made allegations that you stole money from their purses while in Winn Dixie and Piggly Wiggly stores. What is your response to these accusations?"

Lexi put her head down and looked at the floor. Her mom grabbed her hand and squeezed it tight. Lexi looked back up and at the officer.

"I have done all those things, officer."

"Okay. Thank you for your honesty."

Candi interrupted and asked. "Officer, what happens next?"

"At this time, I'm going to make you responsible for her. Basically, she'll be considered under house arrest until further notice. I have this device that she'll have to wear which will monitor her movements and actions."

He knelt down and slipped it onto Lexi's ankle. She was feeling so embarrassed.

"I'll be interviewing each individual who has made a complaint and get a formal written letter of their intention of pressing charges. Once all that is done, you'll be appointed a court counselor from the juvenile court who will schedule a time to meet with you. The counselor will discuss the various charges that have been brought against your daughter. The judge will be given that information to make his determination on what court action is warranted."

"I'll probably go to jail, right?" Lexi asked.

"I can't answer that. All judges are different. Is this the first time you've ever had any indictments against you?"

"Yessir," Lexi replied.

"You being a first-time offender could possibly work on your behalf, but it still doesn't guarantee anything either."

"Officer, how far can my daughter go with the monitor device?"

Officer Hughes answered, "I adjusted it for a five-mile radius. That will give you enough area to go to the store, the nearby park, church, and other locations you might want to go to."

"Thank you very much."

Looking at Lexi, Officer Hughes said. "You're welcome. I hope all goes well and this will be the beginning of you getting back on the right track."

"Yessir," Lexi replied looking so ashamed.

The Sims saw the officer leave and walked back into their home. Candi informed them of her discussion with the officer and the possible scenarios Lexi might have to face. Courtney noticed the device on Lexi's leg and wondered if it was what she thought it was but didn't ask any questions. Lexi was clearly disturbed by the information given her and her mom. Melinda asked them all, "How about I cook some burgers and fries? Does sound okay to everybody?"

"Ralph, would you get the grill started?"

"Sure."

Candi went into the kitchen to help Melinda, which left Lexi and Courtney alone together. Courtney wasn't quite sure how that would turn out.

"What do you think about my new jewelry, Court?"

Courtney didn't know how to answer until she saw a smile appear on her face. They both forced a chuckle.

"I know this has got to be rough, Lexi. I'm so sorry."

"Thanks, cuz, but I brought all this down on myself. I have been so stupid."

"We all do stupid stuff at times, Lexi."

"Yeah, I know, but I think I hit the stupid jackpot."

Again, they both gave an uncomfortable chuckle.

"Hey, Court. I really am sorry for how I've treated you lately. I don't know what happened to me. Mom told me it probably came from all the junk that happened to us over the last couple of years. You know, Dad leaving us, bills piling up on us, and losing our stuff when the house burned down. But it doesn't justify how I've been acting or what I've done."

"Yeah, you're right. You've been a real jerk."

Courtney looked and sounded serious and then giggled. It worried Lexi for a split second but she knew better as soon as she heard Courtney snicker.

"Wow! You about got me there, cuz."

"Look, Lexi. We all can be real jerks and treat people horribly. The difference is the one who does, repents like you're doing. The one that realizes they've been acting horrible and try to make amends can be forgiven."

"Thanks, Court. It's gonna be really tough facing all these people I've wronged. I don't know if I can do it."

"You can't actually. Not without the Lord helping you," Courtney replied.

"Yep, you'd be right. That's all brand-new territory for me."

Courtney continued with some encouraging words. "I learned a verse when I was in the fifth grade. Our Bible teacher told us if we memorized it, she would give each of us a $5.00 Dairy Queen gift certificate. Stupid, huh?"

They both laughed.

"But I'm glad I memorized it. It's in Proverbs 3: 5 and 6. *Trust in the Lord with all your heart. Don't depend on your own understanding. Acknowledge Him in all your ways and He will direct in the way to go.*'"

"Wow! Awesome verse. I need to memorize that."

"Hold on."

Courtney ran back to her bedroom and ran back into the den.

"Can I give you this?"

"It's your Bible, Court. I can't take that."

"Well, actually it's my old Bible and I'd love for you to have it."

Courtney turned to the passage she just shared with Lexi. Lexi read it to herself again. She grabbed Courtney and hugged her.

"You're the best!"

Courtney felt like a million bucks.

They enjoyed the grilled burgers, French fries, and some homemade brownies with ice cream and then watched 'The Chronicles of Narnia: The Lion, the Witch, and the Wardrobe'. Lexi and Candi had never seen it and thoroughly enjoyed it. Lexi commented that she wished there was a sequel to watch.

"Your wish is our command," Ralph answered.

He put in the DVD, 'The Chronicles of Narnia: Prince Caspian'. It was going to be late by the time they finished the second installment, and they usually didn't watch anything that would keep them up so late on a Saturday because they needed their rest to be ready for Sunday services, but this night called for the special occasion. Around 11:30 pm they were getting ready to go to bed when surprisingly enough, Lexi asked her uncle if he would pray for her. They all grabbed hands and Ralph prayed. Courtney couldn't believe how God was working in Lexi's life. So cool, she thought.

Melinda woke up a little later than usual and walked into the kitchen to throw some frozen sausage biscuits into the oven. She was surprised to find her sister sitting at the bar reading her Bible.

"Hi, sis. Hope you don't mind. I made some coffee," Candi said to Melinda.

"Don't mind at all. Thanks much. I'm gonna throw in some sausage biscuits for anyone who might eat one or two."

"Sounds good, Mel. I'll eat one."

"What are you reading?"

"Just some passages in Psalms. I love reading them."

"How's Lexi this morning?"

"Sleeping like a log. I think the medications helped her get the rest she needed."

Ralph came in groaning and stretching. "Coffee! I want coffee, now!"

The ladies laughed at his silliness.

"If you two don't mind, I'd like to join you at church this morning," Candi commented.

"Melinda answered with a smile. "We'd love that. What about Lexi?"

"Umm, I think I'll leave it up to her to make the decision on her own."

"Probably the best, sis."

At that moment Lexi limped in where they were.

"Smells good. Are those your famous sausage biscuits, Aunt Mel?"

"Yeah, so famous they came straight out of the freezer."

They smiled at each other.

"Too bad you can't have one," Ralph said with a serious look. "She only cooked enough for herself, your Mom, and me."

Melinda quickly jumped in and added, "I tell you what, Lexi. You can eat your uncle's and I'll even cook you another one."

They all laughed. Courtney slumbered in and quipped,

"A person can't get any sleep around here for all the noise."

"Glad to see that the dead finally woke up," Courtney's dad joked.

"Lexi, how do you feel this morning?" Courtney asked.

"Still terribly sore, but overall, pretty good. Can you pass me the strawberry jam, please," Courtney slid over the jar and Ralph intercepted it, opened the jar, got a spoonful, and then passed it to Lexi.

Jokingly, Lexi exclaimed, "Well, Uncle Ralph. I've never seen such rudeness in my life. I'm a guest here, you know."

"A guest? Nah, you are family. I can do anything I want to you."

All five laughed. A few minutes went by with little conversation and Lexi commented.

"I guess y'all are going to church this morning. Would there happen to be any room for one more?"

Candi looked up with pride. Ralph, however, had to throw in another tease.

"We were really hoping you would stay home and clean the house and mow the yard."

Melinda went over to Lexi and hugged her. "Absolutely. We'd love for you to go with us."

"Just one thing." Lexi asked. "Can I put bandages around the monitoring device? No one would know the difference. Most, if not all, would think it was one of my injuries."

Melinda answered, "Sounds like a good idea. Come with me and we'll wrap that baby up."

"Thanks, Aunt Mel," Lexi said with gratitude.

Courtney and Lexi planned a little trick to pull on Coco on the way to church. Courtney called Coco.

"Hey, you," Coco answered.

"Hey you, too," Courtney answered.

"Listen. Candi made Lexi come to church this morning so just wanted to make you aware. Don't know how she'll react once she gets there."

"Okay. Thanks for the heads-up."

Courtney got off the phone and smiled at Lexi. When they got inside the church, Coco saw Courtney and Lexi walking together to their classroom.

"Hey Court. Hey Lexi," Coco said.

"What do you want, you little twerp?" Coco looked at Courtney with amazement and didn't know what to say.

Courtney looked at Lexi and said to her, "Lexi! Stop it. When are you ever going to change?"

"How about never, doofus. Why don't you two get outta my face before I…"

At that moment, both Lexi and Courtney looked at Coco and said, "Psych!"

"Wha…!" Coco responded.

They briefly told Coco of the changes the Lord had been making in Lexi's life since the accident. "Oh, I'll get you back. Both of you. Just wait."

They all chuckled on their way to the Bible study class. They walked in and Lexi felt a little awkward, but the Courtneys did everything they could to make her feel comfortable. They introduced her to everyone in the class. Ms. Applin asked everyone to sit down so they could get started.

"Before I start our lesson, I just want to say that it's great to see you here, Lexi. Glad you're feeling better from your accident."

Lexi thanked Ms. Applin.

Ms. Applin continued, "If you have a Bible or a device that has God's Word on it, turn to Proverbs 3:5 – 6."

Lexi turned and looked at Courtney as if she had something to do with this. Courtney pantomimed, "I didn't know she was going to teach on this."

"It's one of my most favorite verses in the Bible. It reads, *"Trust in the Lord with all your heart and don't depend on your own understanding; in all your ways submit to him, and he will make your paths straight."*

Trusting the Lord means putting everything into His hands. They're big enough to handle anything you are going through. Don't depend on your own understanding because we can't see the big picture, but God can. Submitting means holding nothing back. Give it all to Him; your family, schoolwork, future, financials, vocations, everything. And last, but surely not the least, He gives us the promise that He will make our paths straight. Sometimes things just happen because that is just life. This verse applies in that situation. But sometimes we make undesirable choices where this verse still applies. We might have to go through some otherwise difficult times that we might not have had to deal with if we hadn't made such bad decisions. For example, let's say you decided to cheat on an exam. What is crazy is that you took two hours the night before writing the answers down on a small piece of paper to take with you into the classroom when taking the test, when you could have taken that same amount of time to study for the test. But you thought you could slide the paper under your leg and peek at an answer you needed when you got stumped by a question. The next day while taking the test the teacher saw you looking down. She walked to your desk and asked you to stand up. You got caught. She knew that you were cheating. Not only are you embarrassed but you also get a fat zero in your grades. Not a good choice, right? By the way, I have to confess. That's what I did in the eighth grade.

When you make such detrimental decisions, there's nothing you can do but start rebuilding your reputation. Let me take the verse we read and show you how it would apply to your life with this bad choice of you cheating. Trusting the Lord would allow Him to help rebuild your rep. Understand that might mean you will have to make some serious amends, like paying someone back or apologizing to someone or a group. Then you definitely don't want to try and manipulate overhauling your reputation either, because that would be depending on yourself instead of trusting God. And continuing to seek Him for strength and patience during the restoration process of your reputation would be acknowledging Him and seeing, in time, your rep is back to where it was before you made the wrong choice. Is this making sense?"

Coco raised her hand and asked Anna a question.

"So, Ms. Applin, if we do that, are we guaranteed to get our reputation back?"

"Hmm, Coco, I would like to say yes to that question, but there will always be individuals that might not trust you if you deceived them or took something from them that didn't belong to you. But we shouldn't let the response of someone affect us from continuing to rebuild our honor and trustworthiness."

Surprisingly, Lexi raised her hand.

"Yes, Lexi," Anna answered.

"Uh, Ms. Applin, just to be honest, I've made a mess of things since I've been here the last couple of weeks. In fact, the accident I had was because I'd made some really bad decisions. I'm sure I'm going to have to make quite a few paybacks to many people and it scares me to death. Can I be honest?"

"Please do, Lexi."

"I might even have to go to jail."

Courtney, Coco, and the four other girls in the class couldn't believe she was so open and vulnerable.

"Lexi, this is quite brave of you to be so open this morning, but I applaud you and am very proud of you. Most teens would try to hide such feelings."

"I would have, too, a couple of days ago, but the Lord has really been moving me in His direction and I want to make things right."

"Wow, Lexi. What a wonderful choice you're making. Even though I don't know all that has happened and what amends you're going to have to make, I can see how challenging this could be. Sometimes it's very difficult to do the right thing. Trust me, you'll have many times when you don't want to go through with what you know is right. You'll be quick to give it up and think it's not worth it. You might not even feel the presence of the Lord and perhaps feel as if He is far away and not working in the process. But you still are wiser doing what Proverbs 3:5 & 6 tells us. Some situations we have to deal with are much more difficult than others. Would you mind if we all have a prayer for you right now?"

"Please." Anna and the girls held hands and after a few minutes of prayer, Ms. Applin dismissed the class. Lexi thanked Ms. Applin for the instruction and the prayer.

The Courtneys and Lexi went to the church restroom and then into the sanctuary. It was simply incredible to watch the new Lexi taking in the worship experience. Her mother and Courtney's parents were two rows back and if smiling was a crime, all three of them would be given a life sentence. After the preacher finished his message, he gave an altar call to the congregation. He told them to feel welcome to come to the altar and pray if they felt the need. A few went down front and unexpectedly, Lexi slipped out of the pew and walked up to the preacher. They talked for a while and then she came back to her seat next to the Courtneys. Before being dismissed, the preacher spoke.

"A young lady who you have been praying for came down this morning and chatted with me and asked me to tell you that she sincerely appreciated the prayers and thoughts concerning herself and her mother. She asked if we would continue praying because she will be facing some incredibly difficult decisions in the next couple of weeks. I assured her that we would. Let's close in prayer and you can be dismissed."

The families of both Courtneys, Candi, and Lexi went out to eat lunch after church. To 'Wherever.' It was Lexi's idea to go there, and they were a bit surprised, nonetheless, that's where they went. They walked into the establishment and were seated at one of their larger tables. Lexi didn't sit down but instead recognized the waitress that served her the night before her accident. The family watched in anticipation of the transaction between the server and Lexi. They saw the server hug her and then Lexi came back to the table.

"Lexi," Candi asked, "What was that all about?"

"I told her that I was terribly sorry for the rude and disrespectful way I treated her last Friday evening. She's just the first of many restitutions I'm going to need to make."

"Lexi, I'm just amazed at the transformation that has taken place in your life. I'm so proud of you," Lexi's Mom said with pride.

"Thanks, Mom, but I have a long way to go."

"We all do, honey."

Another server came to their table and took their orders. The lunch was tremendous, and the conversations were sensational. Coco and her family went to their home and Courtney, her family, Candi, and Lexi went back to their home.

Lexi knew that they would be passing by the Dollar General store where she had stolen merchandise. She asked her Uncle Ralph if he would mind stopping there for a minute. She wanted to apologize to the clerk if she were there. He pulled into the parking lot, and she got out. The clerk identified her immediately when she walked in.

"Get out! Now! In fact, I'm calling the police right now."

Lexi wasn't expecting this kind of response.

"Please, ma'am. I just wanted to apologize and tell you that I'm willing to do whatever it takes to make things right."

The manager totally ignored Lexi's pleas.

"This is the store manager at the Dollar General. The girl that stole some merchandise is here again. You need to send an officer here. I don't want her in my store. Thank you."

"Ma'am."

"Don't ma'am me, you little thief. The police are on their way right now to throw your butt in jail."

"But ma'am, I was just going…"

"I don't care what you were gonna do or say. Get out and stay out!"

Lexi dropped her head down and walked dejectedly out of the store. She conveyed to her mom what had just transpired. They felt it would be best for them to wait for the police, who arrived within twenty minutes. One of the officers spoke with Candi and Lexi and told them they appreciated the fact that Lexi was trying to make amends, but it would probably be best to wait until the court decides is the best way to handle her offenses. The store manager came outside and spoke to the officer.

"What? You're not going to arrest her?"

"We already did last week and she's out on probation."

"You need to have her butt in jail. That's where she belongs. The hoodlum!"

"We're handling it, ma'am."

The officer told Lexi and her mother to get back in the vehicle and go back home. Ralph put the car in reverse and pulled out of the parking lot. Lexi was uncontrollably weeping.

"All I wanted to do was tell her I was sorry and that I will pay them back as soon as I can."

"I know, honey, but there are going to be some people who just aren't going to accept your apologies right now. They are going to be skeptical of you. It's going to take time."

"It's not fair, mom."

"Honey, how would you feel toward someone who stole something from you? Would you be quick to believe them if they came to you after you had found out they had done it?"

Lexi hesitated for a moment and then responded.

"I see your point. I just didn't know it was going to be this hard."

Candi hugged her daughter as Lexi leaned her head on her mom's shoulder and continued to cry.

Candi received a call early Monday morning while she was eating some cereal and reading her Bible.

"Hello. This is her. Yes ma'am. Uh-huh, I understand. Meet you today at 10:00 and then tomorrow at 1:00 we'll go before the judge. Thank you, Ms. Ross. We'll see you in a couple of hours."

It was their counselor from the juvenile court. They were trying to handle cases that were on their docket, and they wanted to schedule Lexi's case. What Candi didn't know was that Officer Hughes happened to be at the church they attended the day before and appreciated the display of Lexi's attitude and demeanor. He didn't see that very often in his vocation, so he put in a good word for them with the judge, who was a good friend and he happened to play golf with every week.

After sharing with the judge about the obvious change in Lexi, the only favor Officer Hughes asked was if he would expedite Lexi's case since, they lived out of town and needed to get back to some kind of normalcy.

Candi finished reading Psalm chapter nine and reread verse nine for comfort. *"The Lord is a stronghold for the oppressed, a stronghold in times of trouble."*

"Thank You, Lord. Please help us through today. Give Lexi strength, courage, and humility to handle the situation. Please give the judge the wisdom that is necessary and May You be glorified through it all and please be our stronghold. We will trust You with the outcome. I love You, Lord,"

Candi woke up Lexi and told her about the call with the counselor and how they needed to get a move on to make it by 10:00.

After Lexi's sleep, her body was stiff, and she felt every painful motion. Her mom helped her wash her hair and get her clothes on. As humbling as it was for self-confident, do-it-yourself Lexi, she was thoroughly enjoying the attention her mom was giving her. Courtney woke up and threw some bread into the toaster and noticed that her Aunt and cousin were shuffling around in the guest room, so she yelled out if they wanted her to fix them anything. Lexi straggled into the kitchen and said no thanks. "Mom got a call from my court counselor, and we have to meet with her at 10:00. We might be able to get something at Hardee's on the way."

Courtney asked, "After that, what will happen, Lexi?"

"Mom said the counselor will give the judge all the information for him to make the judgment. We meet with him tomorrow at 1:00."

"Wow! Seems as if things are really moving fast."

"Yeah, and I'm glad. The waiting is a killer."

"I'll be praying for y'all today. I love you, cuz."

Lexi stopped and stared at Courtney for a few seconds and then walked to her and gave her the biggest hug she'd gotten in a long time.

"Courtney, I don't think anyone in this world has a better cousin."

Courtney gave her a big smile and replied, "Yeah. You'd be right."

They both chuckled. Candi rushed through the room, said hi to Courtney, grabbed her purse and, then told Lexi they needed to get into the car.

"Love y'all!" Courtney yelled to them as they drove away.

They pulled away from the Sim's home, had just enough time to grab two biscuits, coffee, and cola at Hardee's, and then headed to the courthouse. They parked on the second floor of the large parking deck and walked to the elevator. The sign next to it explained where they needed to go. Juvenile court, third floor. They weren't sure where exactly to go and asked a lady walking down the hall if she knew where they would find room 333. The lady told them it was just around the corner. They opened the door and there sat Ms. Ross. She told them to come in and once they sat down, she proceeded to tell Lexi and her mom that she had contacted the women who Lexi had stolen money from and each one told Ms. Ross that they would not continue to press charges as long as Lexi pays them back. The Dollar General store surprisingly said the same but with one stipulation. Lexi was not allowed to go into that particular store again.

"Lexi, do you remember the items you stole? I need for you to be as exact as possible."

"Yes ma'am. I think I do. A pair of sunglasses, two pairs of panties, two jersey-type shirts, two pairs of workout shorts, two pairs of socks, two beers, and two sandwiches. I think that's all."

"Okay. I'll be calling them to ask what the cost is, and you'll need to pay it back this week."

"Yes ma'am. I understand. Umm, Ms. Ross? I did some other things that I need to tell you about."

"Okay, what would that be?"

"Well, one morning I ate breakfast at the Main Street Café and after eating most of it, I placed a cockroach under a piece of bacon and acted as if I had just found it in my food. They apologized and told me I didn't have to pay for my meal. Then the first night I stayed at the 24/7 fitness center I stole some shorts and a shirt out of somebody's locker. I also stole some merchandise from the Hibbett's Sporting Goods store one evening."

The counselor looked at Lexi and the news didn't surprise her at all. She'd seen it all before. The counselor responded. "Lexi, I appreciate you telling me about these other issues, but they're not going to be part of the court's issues. Those are personal situations you and your mom need to discuss and handle the best way you see fit."

Candi had a few other questions, which Ms. Ross was able to answer most of them except the question on how the judge would rule.

They were in the meeting for about an hour and a half. Candi and Lexi felt a little relief but knew there was still a rocky road ahead. They had to pay back those she had stolen from, and of course, still had to go before the judge. Candi suggested they get some Kentucky Fried Chicken and ride a few miles up the Natchez Trace for a picnic. It's a 444-mile recreational road and scenic drive through three states. A historic travel corridor used by American Indians, "Kaintucks," European settlers, slave traders, soldiers, and future presidents. Today, many people enjoy not only a scenic drive but also hiking, biking, horseback riding, and camping along the Parkway. They stopped occasionally to look at a rolling stream, or at an overlook of some rock structure. They even read some of the tourist road signs and went into some of the tourist shops. They both fully enjoyed every minute of their time together. At one of the overlooks, they held hands and prayed that the Lord would take them through the rough waters ahead. It was a great mother and daughter day and a long time needed.

Courtney went over to Coco's home and informed her and her mom of about the recent events.

"Hey, Coco, where's your sling?"

"The doc said I didn't have to wear it unless I started to feel some discomfort. He said to put it back on if I did."

"Hmm, Ms. Lawrence, I wonder if Ms. Stubborn over here will do that?"

Coco gave Courtney the stink eye.

Coco then replied, "I learned my lesson, Courtney. I'm not gonna be stupid again. Now you on the other hand probably would be."

"Alright you two, go do something. You're getting on my last nerve."

They all laughed.

Chapter Nineteen: Judgment Day

Lexi and her mom were planning on leaving for the juvenile court at noon to ensure that nothing would interfere with the 1 o'clock appointment with the judge. Both had been nervous wrecks all morning. They must have prayed together two or three times. While at work, Melinda and Ralph texted Candi that they too were praying for the meeting. Courtney did her best to help them endure the time before the appointment by talking about other things, playing some games with Lexi on their Play Station, and watching a Harry Potter movie but the afternoon appointment weighed too heavy on their minds. Finally, it was time to leave. Candi and Lexi arrived at the courthouse at 12:30 and met Ms. Ross in her office. She talked with them and prepared them for the various actions the judge could order.

They walked into the courtroom and sat down. Within a few minutes, Lexi was called to the judge's bench.

"Are you Lexi Patterson?"

"Yessir."

"Do you know why you are here today?"

"Yessir."

"My understanding is you have been accused of stealing personal property from individuals and merchandise from a local store. Is that correct?"

"Sir, if you mean the four ladies I stole money from in the grocery stores, and the items I took at the Dollar General, yessir, that is correct."

"So, you are in agreement with the court that you have committed the crimes that have been charged against you?"

"Yessir."

"Ms. Patterson, if your records are correct, you haven't ever been in this kind of trouble before, correct?"

"Yessir. That is correct."

"Why now? What caused you to begin going down this path of destructive behavior?"

Lexi looked down at her feet for a moment then she looked back up and answered the judge. "I don't want to make excuses for myself but if I were forced to give a reason, I would say my rebellion started when my dad and mom broke up a year ago and mom had to be gone so often to work to pay the bills. Also, just a few weeks ago our trailer burned down and my mom and I lost everything we owned. I kept getting madder and madder at everyone and everything in my life. I even got mad at God. I know that doesn't make it okay for what I've done but like I said, if I had to give a reason, I guess that would be it."

"So, Ms. Patterson, what makes you think you would be any different once you made recompense to those you stole from and maybe even spent some time in detention?"

Lexi dropped head again and this time waited a little longer for her answer. "Judge, I think the accident I was in made a huge impression on my life, but more importantly, and I hesitate to say this because you probably hear it all the time, but God has been making some radical changes in my life that I thought would never happen. Life has been quite difficult over the last two years, but my mom and I have reunited and she, too, has given her life back to the Lord. We both have a very different outlook on things, and I believe we'll be able to move past these horrible choices I've made these past two weeks once I make restitution to those I've harmed."

"Ms. Ross and Lexi's mom, would you two please step up here?"

Candi and Ms. Ross walked up to the judge's bench and the judge looked at Candi and asked, "Ms. Patterson, do you feel you would be able to manage your daughter now and would be able to keep her from making such terrible choices?"

"Yessir, I do."

The judge stared straight at Candi for what seemed like thirty minutes but in reality, it was only two or three seconds. He then looked at Ms. Ross and asked.

"Ms. Ross, what is your evaluation of this young lady and what would your recommendation be?"

"Sir, I've only known Lexi for two days. I'm not sure I'm qualified to make any recommendations."

"For grins and giggles, Ms. Ross, what is your gut feeling about her?"

Ms. Ross hesitated long enough to gather her thoughts and answered. "I personally think that Lexi is sincere in making retribution and I feel that she has truly made a 180-degree turn."

"What gives you that indication?"

"During our session yesterday after I'd confronted her with the criminal actions that were being brought up against her, she quickly took ownership of her actions and even told me of some other actions she had committed that no one would have ever known about if she hadn't told me. She felt the need to confess them to me and proceeded to ask me what she should do about them."

"Are they worth bringing to the court's attention, Ms. Ross?"

"No sir, I don't think so. She also went to the Dollar General store yesterday to apologize to the store manager and tell her that she would pay her back as soon as she could. She told me of a scam at a restaurant where she got a free meal, too."

He looked at Lexi and spoke. "Ms. Patterson, do you realize just how far you were traveling down this road of devastation and ruin in such a short time?"

"Yessir."

The judge leaned back in his huge recliner chair, folded his hands behind his head, and asked Lexi what she thought he should do to her. Lexi was a little caught off guard with his question and after a brief pause, fighting back tears, she answered him.

"Sir, I'm guilty of all these things. I'm extremely embarrassed. When I take a moment and look back, I can't believe I've done them. I'm terribly sorry and want to pay each person back for what I took. I deserve punishment, judge, I know that for sure. I think you are the only one in position that can make such a decision and whatever that decision will be, I've already accepted it as God's will, and I will live with it."

The judge told all three to step back and go to their seats. They did so as the judge studied the papers in front of him. After several minutes he told Lexi to step up before him again. She slid out of the seats they were sitting on and walked to his bench and looked into his face.

"Ms. Patterson, I see hundreds of cases every year where juveniles like you, have made damaging and detrimental choices that have wrecked their lives. Most of them, sad to say, don't learn from their wrongful decisions and continue making a total mess of their lives and everyone around them. I tend to believe that these years of experience behind this bench have made me pretty good at determining whether or not an individual is being sincere and honest. I believe you are one of those individuals. You were correct when you said that the unfortunate recent experiences in yours and your mom's lives do not justify your lack of good judgment and horrific actions but at the same time, it's understandable how horrible events can cause an individual to do things that they would normally never do. Ms. Patterson, my ruling on your behalf is based on my instincts and also that you are a first-time offender. Let's keep it that way. You will stay on house arrest for one more week starting this coming Monday. During this time, you will come to this courthouse and will work from 8:00 am to 5:00 pm with the maintenance staff. You'll be doing janitorial duties and ground maintenance. At the end of the week, you will meet with Ms. Ross, who will evaluate your progress. She will then send me that report for my evaluation. In addition to that, those you stole from must be repaid at the end of the week. If there are any incongruities during the week, for instance, tardiness on your arrival for work, bad attitude, or negative behavior while you work or the individuals you stole from haven't been repaid, then I will reconvene with you and will consider placing you into a home for juvenile delinquents for a period of time I deem necessary. Do you have any questions, Ms. Patterson?"

"No sir."

"Ms. Patterson, the judge asking Lexi's mother, do you have any questions, and do you understand my decision?"

"Yessir, I do."

"Ms. Ross, any questions"

"No sir."

"Thank you all. You're dismissed."

Ms. Ross, Candi, and Lexi gathered together outside the courtroom. Ms. Ross spoke.

"Lexi, do you have any questions for me?"

"No ma'am."

"So, you understand what you have to do this next week?"

"Yes ma'am."

"Ms. Patterson, any questions?"

"I don't think so. At least not at this time. Would you agree that this turned out pretty good?" Candi asked Ms. Ross.

"Most definitely. I think the judge was extremely lenient. He could have been much harder in his decision."

"Thank you. Ms. Ross. We appreciate all you have done."

"Yes, thank you, Ms. Ross." Lexi reiterated.

"You're both very welcome. Let's work through next week, get all this behind you, and begin with a fresh start."

Candi and Lexi both nodded in agreement. They drove back to her sister and brother-in-law's home. Melinda was just about to pull out the roast she put into the crock pot that morning and Courtney was setting the table.

"Hey, girls. We want to hear all about your day and how everything went. Supper will be ready in about fifteen minutes. Y'all haven't eaten already, have you?" Melinda asked.

"No and can't wait to dig into that roast beef. It smells awesome," Candi answered. "We'll clean up a little and during supper, we'll tell you all the news."

"Perfect."

They all sat down for a scrumptious supper and Candi and Lexi told them everything the judge had ordered.

Ralph interjected and jokingly said, "You mean we have to put up with you two for another week? Ahh."

"Honey, I've got an idea. Why don't you stay at the YMCA while we girls stay together all week alone?"

"Real funny, Mel."

All of them laughed.

Epilogue: It Is Finished

The next week Lexi worked every day just like she was supposed to. She was at the courthouse at 7:45 every morning. By the end of the week, the groundskeeper supervisor told Ms. Ross that he wished he had ten more like Lexi. He said she was one of the hardest workers he's ever had. The janitorial supervisor said the exact same thing except she said she wished she had twenty like her. Paying back those she had stolen was more difficult to handle. Neither Candi nor Lexi had the funds to repay the people back. Ralph and Melinda said they would be glad to give them the money. Lexi told them she was extremely grateful for the notion, but she would rather them lend it to her and allow her to pay it back as soon as they got resettled in Tupelo. She said she'd babysit, do yard work, and other odd jobs until she pays them back. They agreed to her proposition. Lexi met with each individual who she had stolen from, repaid them in full and apologized for her horrible behavior. They all seemed to believe her and seemed appreciative, as well. Even the Dollar General Store manager said she was grateful that Lexi had actually followed through with her responsibility and mentioned that she could see an actual change in her. She asked her what made her change, which gave Lexi a perfect opportunity to share how Jesus had used the accident and everything else to get her attention.

The week went by pretty fast and there were some thrilling events that had occurred. Candi had received great news from the insurance company the day before. They were going to be able to purchase another home as soon as they got back. Kenny Parker, the pastor from Christ Community, dropped by the Sim's home. He met Candi and told her that the church had been gathering donations for them. They had received various clothes for both of them, kitchen supplies, toiletries, bedroom furniture, and living room furniture. One family even donated a washer and dryer. Pastor Parker also gave her a check from the church's benevolent fund for $1000.00. Candi broke down into tears. She couldn't believe the church had been so gracious to them. He told her that they would even bring the items to them once they had settled into their new home in Tupelo.

Another exciting event happened on Saturday morning. Officer Hughes came by the Sims' house and gave Candi and Lexi the good news that he'd be taking the ankle monitor off Lexi's ankle. He also gave them papers that showed Lexi had completed her requirements from the judge and now she was free from any incriminating charges. All the family were elated, to say the least. And what surprised everyone more than anything was an interesting call Candi received from her ex-husband. He asked if she would meet with him. Suspiciously she asked what he wanted to talk about, he told her an unbelievable story.

A few weeks ago, he'd met a young man at the construction site where he was working. They became pretty good friends, and the young man invited him to his church. He didn't know why he decided to go, but when he did, it started a chain reaction in his life that he never thought would happen. He and the lady he was living with broke up and He asked Christ to come and be the Lord of his life and make any changes that needed to be made. He stopped drinking and started reading the Bible.

Candi, of course, was somewhat skeptical and had some reservations, yet excited at the possibility of them being a family again. She told him that she'd meet with him eventually but first, she had to get some other issues settled. Candi wasn't going to rush into the relationship, and she definitely wasn't going to tell Lexi about her conversation with him. At least, not yet. She would wait for an opportune time for that to take place.

Everybody hugged each other and said their goodbyes. It had been an interesting three weeks, that's for sure. Candi and Lexi weren't a hundred yards down the road when their car stopped. Lexi got out and ran toward Courtney.

"Court, I almost forgot. I meant to give this back to you a couple of days ago and totally forgot. I hope you can forgive me for taking it."

It was Courtney's favorite ring that her grandmother had given her. Courtney grabbed Lexi around the neck and hugged her.

"Thank you, Lexi. I love you."

Lexi turned and headed back to their car, and they drove back to Tupelo. At that same time, Courtney's phone rang.

"Hey, you."

"Hey, you. Guess what I just found out."

"What?"

"I might have one of the best cousins in the world."

Coco responded. "Yep. I would agree. And, of course, you have the best friend in the world, too."

"Well, maybe!" Courtney jokingly replied.

www.ingramcontent.com/pod-product-compliance
Lightning Source LLC
Chambersburg PA
CBHW032259310726
48973CB00008B/2455